So...
THIS
Happened

A COMEDY OF HORRORS

BOOK ONE

By
David Partelow

Cover by OliviaProDesign

ISBN: 9781694845429

DEDICATION

Quite simply, this book is dedicated to the readers.

For the ones that always pushed me to keep going, the ones that pressed me for more, the ones who wrote and reviewed and offered me their thoughts and continue to support me to this day, I must say humbly, thank you. You make me love to tell these stories and press on to offer new adventures again and again.

ACKNOWLEDGMENTS

I would love to acknowledge the journey that became this book. This story and its expanding adventures returned me from the worst writer's block I had ever known. Since then, I have never looked back. And while this particular storyline is crude, insane, and wrong in so many ways, I must always acknowledge what it did for me and be grateful. That was the utmost point. I had no idea what to expect or where I was heading when I wrote this. I just know that I sincerely laughed out loud often and had one hell of a time. And while this book is the new beginning to that story, the gratitude for it rings true, for it has shown me that this tale and its crazy band of goobers are never far from my heart.

It is my sincere hope that you enjoy this tale as much as I have. It is all sorts of wrong in all the right ways. And with that admission I can say that you've been properly warned. And if you choose to judge me or question my sanity at the end of this book, please know I already am well aware of my situation, so yeah.

1

A MOST AWKWARD SECOND COMING

An ancient being older than recorded time walked through the city, surveying the progress of mankind. Garbed like a homeless vagabond as he was, none that passed him paid him any mind. It was easy to turn a nose up at him and not comprehend the unbridled power the being possessed or the vast knowledge he contained. The being watched the passing humans morosely, feeling deeply equal parts of pain and rejection.

He was, in truth, their creator after all.

Well, co-creator really.

Details.

The being had gone by many monikers in his day, but first and foremost, he was Adam. Now Adam had dabbled in many forays in legend and godhood, hoping to guide his creations upon a righteous path through the ages. For it was he who had gifted humanity with free will, believing it was mankind who should carve their fate and not be some mindlessly devoted bit of flesh and bone. And it was Adam who still believed in his creations now through all trial and tribulation.

And it was a belief and a love that had often bitten Adam gloriously upon the ass over countless centuries.

As Adam walked now, he reflected on a myriad of missteps, feeling deeply of remembrance and pain. He pulled the poncho closer to his body, keeping up the charade. Adam preferred nameless hobo these days, for it matched the melancholy he often felt. Humanity would look on him as a leper, oblivious to the chiseled Adonis that lurked underneath the charade. But Adam was a being of love and understanding, and his children were born of his image. This fact made it difficult for him to reconcile the self-absorbed fuckery that floundered about him incessantly.

Adam may have been the alien to Earth, but it was his creations that seemed foreign to him now. The air felt positively butt-humped by the pollution continuously coughing out of the vehicles relentlessly meandering back and forth. And the love affair these humans had with their cellular devices was the most bone chilling of all. Most of them passing by Adam were fixated upon these screens as they either played some game or kept up some image or judged another on what was called "social media." Adam watched as an attractive woman left a local coffee bistro before taking what they called a "selfie" of her and her beverage before clearly posting it to the interwebs. The woman was so absorbed with it she nearly bumped into Adam, and Adam knew had she connected with him, she gladly would have rested the blame on his shoulders.

Adam watched these things with grim, pained eyes. The division, the self-absorption, the gluttonous misery that permeated the lives of those before him, well it was all enough to further his sadness. Adam realized he had failed his creations somehow. Yet for the eternal life of him he couldn't figure out just where he had gone wrong. Adam had assumed many forms for his creatures, from benevolent gods to loving messiahs, and every attempt had eventually blown up gloriously in his face. Adam felt a tinge of pain from his last loving foray, when mankind had crucified him for his attempts at love and salvation.

Complicated, fickle fuckers they were.

Adam examined the scars on his hands. He could have easily willed them away, yet he chose to keep them as a reminder. His "return" three days later had done some good for a while, but that too eventually faded. Adam knew mankind still needed guidance, but what stymied him time and time again was how selfish, greedy souls could turn his messages into a weapon for their own gain. Adam realized that this selfish minority had cost countless lives in the end, much to his utter dismay.

The heavy thoughts of these matter distracted Adam enough that he didn't see the man in his path until it was too late. Not looking up from his phone, the man collided fully with Adam. The veiled deity did his best to stumble back appropriately for the impact, looking sorry for the endeavor. The man, looking like he had just left a sporting event, adorned in a blaze of red to support his team, was immediately angry.

"I am terribly sorry, sir," said Adam apologetically.

The man obviously chose not to hear him as his chest puffed and he huffed with bravado. Adam discovered many of his male creations often fought the dreaded demon of overcompensation. "Why don't you watch where the fuck you're going, dickweed," he said, obviously wanting some confrontation.

Adam, eternally patient, kept his composure. “This is completely unnecessary. As I said before, I am sorry. I will just be on my way now,” he replied.

“The fuck you will,” said the man, blocking Adam’s departure. “You apologize like you mean it while you still got teeth, you god damn bum.”

“How very, droll,” said Adam as he tried to go around once more.

The man blocked his way again. “So, you’re too good to apologize *and* work, you good for nothing shit bag?”

Adam could easily smell the man’s boozy breath as a crowd formed. Apparently, the prospect of a fist fight was still enough to pull people from their phones. Adam watched a large vein protrude from the man’s head. From a bystander’s standpoint, they were evenly matched in height and build. Some people had turned on the cameras of their devices hoping to record something that could go viral.

The man looked around at the gathering masses and was bolstered by it. “Are ya deaf too, ya fucking bum?” he asked, raising his voice for greater effect.

Adam shook his head softly. “No, just greatly disappointed in you acting like a petulant child,” he said.

The man held out his hands. “Oh, you fucking did it now,” he said as he squared up in a fighting stance, wobbling a bit as he did.

Adam looked at the crowd in disbelief as they egged it on. “This is what you like now?” he asked no one, everyone.

As Adam looked at the assembling crowd, the man took a swing at him. The fist connected with Adam’s jaw. The crowd made sympathetic sounds at the sound of breaking. Adam turned to look at the man clutching at his broken knuckle. Shaking his head again, Adam grabbed him by the jersey he wore.

"Well, you are sober now, aren't you?" asked Adam as he regarded the man. "Why couldn't you just listen?"

The man's fear hadn't caught up fully with his pride yet, as he still pandered to the crowd. "Imma fuck you up, man," he stammered through the pain.

Adam shook his head. "Hardly, child, for I created you, I certainly know all the ways to stop you," he said.

"The fuck you-" was all the man got out before Adam went to work.

With blinding speed Adam's other hand sped across the man, tapping him soundly in three places on his chest and then once upon his neck. Adam then finished with a tap upon his forehead. The man stammered back, his eyes rolling as he fought to remain on his feet. The man then puked on the crowd as he colored the back of his pants with a solid brown. The crowd jumped back as the man coated those close to him before falling to the ground in a deep, blissful sleep.

Gazing on the gawking crowd, Adam motioned with his hands. Every cell phone present hissed and squawked before their screens burnt out. Many of the bystanders dropped their phones as they turned and fled. Adam watched them go, further dismayed by their actions as he continued walking down the street.

Now alone once more, Adam lost himself in further contemplation. Surely with all the damage to the cellular devices someone had alerted the authorities. Adam thought it best to lay low. He ducked into a small coffeehouse, welcoming the inviting aroma of coffee beans, one of the greatest scents upon Earth.

To Adam's relief, the coffeehouse was local. He didn't bother with the name, but he relished in the genuine feel of a non-chain with its soothing, retro feel and deep, rich caffeination brewing from behind the counter. The café was moderately filled with patrons sipping on warm beverages, either carrying on conversations or glued to computer screens. There was always a serene beauty to coffeehouses to Adam, and he welcomed the scent and familiarity openly.

"Ah, coffee. One of the few creations I got absolutely right," he breathed before walking to the counter.

Upon seeing him, the gal behind the counter winced before putting on a fake smile. The smile was pleasant to look upon, even through the metal that adorned the woman's lips and nose. Adam made a note of her tattoos and vibrantly purple hair as he approached her. "What can I get for you?" she asked.

Adam began to rummage in his pockets. "Coffee, please. Black and pure as the night," he said.

The lady turned to pour him a cup, offering polite, stale conversation. "You look like you've had a rough night," she said.

"A rough life really," said Adam distantly. "I am still trying to figure it all out and just exactly where I went wrong."

"That can take a life time," said the woman.

"And then some," said Adam with a wry grin.

The lady turned back and placed a big, steamy mug of liquid gold upon the counter. She then waved Adam away. "It's on me, tonight," she said freely.

"That is not necessary," said Adam.

The woman shrugged. "Hey, we all need a pick-me-up sometime," she replied.

Adam took the coffee in his hands, nodding to the woman. "You have my thanks," he said. "I won't forget your kindness."

"Don't mention it," said the woman.

Adam turned from her and found an empty table and sat down, smelling the contents of his cup. His nostrils welcomed the fragrance, invigorating his senses. Coffee was perfect as is in his eyes, and such a concoction was ruined with unnecessary additions. Things like vanilla and hazelnut merely detracted from that glory.

Adam was at least thankful it wasn't pumpkin spice season.

Sipping his coffee, Adam set his focus upon the TV on the corner wall. A newscaster went about his duties as even more news scrolled on the screen below him. Dire news littered the screen, a trend that had only worsened as of late. It was a trend that only compounded mankind's problems in the end.

As he stared blankly at the TV, the lady behind the counter came up to his table. "Do you need anything else?" she asked.

Adam motioned to the empty chair at his little table. "Just some company if you have a moment," he replied.

The woman looked at the counter and shrugged before sitting down. "What the hell," she said. "You seem harmless enough."

Adam watched the woman sit and regard him as he sipped his coffee. He said nothing at first, admiring how brave she was, for most people grew uncomfortable with his presence over time. "If I may ask, what is your name?"

"Kelly," she said as she rested her elbows on the table. "And you are?"

"Adam," he said absently. "You can call me Adam," he replied.

Kelly nodded. "Very well, Adam. If you don't mind me asking, why so glum? You look like you have the weight of the world on your shoulders."

Adam chuckled at this lightly. "In some ways I do, I suppose. Let's just say my life is…complicated."

Kelly regarded him and his words. “Fair enough,” she said. “Do you have a place to stay tonight? I mean, are you going to be okay?”

Adam smiled at her. “I am always alright, Kelly. Don’t you worry about me. I think there are enough things to worry about right now to be quite honest,” he said.

Kelly nodded. “Yeah, it’s looking pretty fucked up out there lately. People keep saying that the assholes spouting about the Mayan Calendar end of times might be right this time,” she said distantly.

Adam chuckled at this. “It won’t be the first or last time you hear about it,” said Adam.

Kelly shrugged. “I don’t know. It feels kinda real these days. Hell, even the government is taking action this time,” she said.

“How do you mean?” asked Adam.

She pointed to the TV. “You didn’t hear? They are implementing a new vaccine. They call it Omega. They created it from the components of a newly discovered element in Mexico. They say it has tremendous healing properties. The first shipments are supposed to be here by the end of the week,” she said.

“And where was this discovery made?” asked Adam.

Kelly chewed on her lip a minute. “In Mexico…the Yucatán I think,” she said.

Adam put his coffee down, lowing his head. “Well shit,” he said.

“What is it?” Kelly asked.

Adam stood, walked over and stood directly in front of the TV. Sure enough, he could read about the Omega Vaccine as the scrolling text offered info and locations to get vaccinated. His thoughts went to the Chichén Itzá archeological dig site and what was hidden there. Mankind was not supposed to find that, much less fuck with it as they did.

"Shit," said Adam again, shaking his head. "And the holiest of shits I dare say." The supreme being then proceeded to bang his head repeatedly upon the little table.

"Um, Adam?" asked Kelly hovering nearby, looking at him like he was crazy.

Adam stopped to look at her gravely. "It appears that I was mistaken, Kelly. Things don't appear bad. Things *are* bad," he said as he reached into his pockets and handed her a one hundred-dollar bill. "I think it is time you go enjoy yourself, Kelly. Go out tonight. Have some fun. Make a lasting memory. Make the most of these moments because quite soon things will no longer be the same," said Adam.

"Um, thanks," said Kelly tried to figure out what was going on. "What exactly are you going on about?"

Adam made his way to the door before he turned back regard Kelly again. "I cannot say, but I can say this, Kelly. Whatever you do, don't get that vaccine," he said before he left.

Kelly watched him go, confused by the exchange. The woman thought on Adam's words and actions. She looked at the TV, and then to where Adam had just departed and then at the money in her hand. Pocketing the money, Kelly shook her head and returned to behind the counter once more.

"Yeah, I knew he was fucking crazy," she mumbled before going back to work.

Back outside, Adam walked with quick steps, determined to act at once. Yet the ancient deity paused after a few blocks, realizing he hadn't the foggiest notion as to what the hell to do next. If the Omega vaccine was world-wide, then there was little he could do. It was free will, and the very notion of it was about to bitch-slap him with serious authority.

"Maybe this is it. Maybe the time has come," he said before shaking his head bitterly. "God damnit. I thought we had a few thousand more years before things went to hell," he said.

Still muttering under his breath about the magnitude of the approaching shitstorm, Adam walked again into the night.

2

A DAY IN THE DAY OF

Brandon Andrew Morgan felt the impending alarm before he heard it. He knew it was time to wake, dreaded it in fact, and wanted that extra thirty seconds of rest. Yet, despite the warmth of his covers, Brandon felt the cold bleakness of reality ready and waiting to leap upon him like a cat. An evil cat. An evil cat on catnip while also in heat. The day beckoned to him mercilessly and he wished he could give no fucks about it whatsofriggingever.

Yet he was the responsible one.

Always the responsible one.

Fucking details.

Sitting up with a series of groans, Brandon placed his feet upon the floor. Rubbing at his eyes and unleashing a Chewbacca-like yawn, he looked at himself in the mirror from across the room. Everything in the reflection was quite neat looking and an image of order save for him. He scowled at his image as he motivated himself to move.

"Well, fuck you," he said to himself in protest. "And fuck you too," he replied as well since he was talking to himself after all.

Brandon sulked walk his way to the bathroom, turning on the shower to as hot as his skin would allow. Undressing, he stepped into the running water, ready for it to wash over him and revive his senses. Brandon then screamed like a banshee in heat, for the shower was devoid of all warmth. Realizing his roommate had used it all primping himself most likely, Brandon jumped in and out of the water long enough to get wet, partially soaped up, and shampooed before he hovered under the water until he was cleansed, focusing on his inadvertent tormentor as he did.

"God damnit, Josh, you metrosexual fuck!" he bellowed before fleeing the shower abruptly. Sometimes it sucked having roommates.

At least he was clean.

Sorta.

Again, fucking details.

Shuffling back to his room with a towel around his waist, Brandon checked his clock before getting dressed. He unfortunately had more than enough time to deal with unnecessary bullshit before he started his day at work. It felt like it never ended. Brandon loved where he worked, but mall patrons sometimes had a way of running even the best of things through a field of festering turds. That being said, he never discounted the fact that at least he got paid to put up with their shit.

Now dressed in blue jeans, a long sleeve gray shirt and his work shirt, Brandon was just about ready to face the day. As he styled his short, nigh black hair, he judged himself incessantly. As males went, Brandon was attractive, always smelled good, and kept clean. The problem was he had a kindness about him that put him low on the bad-boy scale and made him cute but not in the category of hot. As salsa's went, he was on the mild end: a safe choice with his romantic flair and easy-going nature. But often his failed relationships ended because his ex-girlfriends wanted a little more spice.

But if you asked Brandon, he was more than willing to tell you where Cosmo could kiss it.

Thus prepared and armed, Brandon took a deep breath and prepped to depart his room. Boldly striding forward, he ventured into the living room to assess the damage from the night before. Gratefully, things were not as bad as they could have been, but obviously there had been some late-night gaming on the PlayStation. The guilty parties had been gracious enough to focus the glorious mess around the vicinity of the TV, making clean up minimal and less annoying than usual.

With the area hastily cleaned, Brandon turned his attention to preparing breakfast. Starting a pot of coffee, Brandon then procured his breakfast items from the fridge. Starting a tray of bacon in the oven, he proceeded to beat and season eggs before scrambling them. When the coffee was done dripping, he poured the coffee back into the pot and started to brew it again. Coffee once through the pot was for amateurs.

Setting the apartment's little table, Brandon sat down and made himself a plate. That was his payment for his work, first dibs on the food. If the others didn't like it, they were more than welcome to cook their own or go fuck themselves. This sentiment was mostly an unspoken rule that everyone just sorta understood. Besides, Brandon was the best cook of the group. He took a bite of his cheese smothered eggs, relishing the flavor and the solitude that accompanied it.

That, of course, lasted about as long as premature ejaculator in a porn flick.

Bursting from their shared room in glorious fashion came Brandon's best friends Joshua and Sarah. The two had dated for even longer than they had known Brandon and were inseparable. This of course didn't mean they didn't argue over anything and everything under the sun, and they took that very moment to prove it. Brandon knew it was most likely for the make-up sex.

It was almost always for the make-up sex.

If you were to look up "loveable jock" on the internet, it would be a surprise if Joshua's face didn't immediately pop up. He stood a cocky six feet tall and had a smile and swagger that made women swoon and men want to just slap the ever-loving shit out of him. Yet, despite his dashing looks, excessive primping, and macho swagger, underneath all of that was a loveable son of a bitch.

And in terms of beauty, Sarah was a looker herself. Curvy in all the right ways, she had shimmering eyes and soft, pouty lips that got her way many a time. What made her dangerous and a foil for Joshua was she was also sharp as a tack. She was brushing her long, golden hair as she trailed Joshua, obviously annoyed by his stubbornness.

Shaking his head, Josh spoke as he walked to the table. "Look, babe, you know I am all for health and what not, but this just sounds crazy to me. We should know a bit more about it before we take the plunge is all I'm saying," he said.

Sarah was unmoved, rolling her eyes as she brushed. "You are going, and that is final. I am not taking any chances this year. I let you bitch out of the flu shot last season and that came back to bite all of our asses," she said.

"Mostly mine," mumbled Brandon between bites.

Josh walked over to the table, taking a piece of bacon and relishing a bite before nodding to Brandon. “Morning, bro,” he said before turning back to Sarah. “I don’t think I’m being a dick by wanting more info on something before I get it injected into me,” he told her.

Narrowing her eyes, Sarah responded darkly. “Well if you want to inject me again, I suggest you get it, fast,” she said before smiling in all sweetness at the table. “Morning, Brandon!”

“Hey,” said Brandon as he watched the two lovers in their spat. Much of his entertainment derived from observing such displays. For the moment, he was but a fixture in the apartment. Once they were finished, he would exist in their world again. Until then, he had his own reality show.

Josh threw up his hands before taking one more bite of the bacon. “Fuck, babe, that’s just cold. Criminal even. Don’t you think, B?” he asked.

Brandon shook his head as he stuffed another bite in his mouth. “Oh, I know better than to jump on that grenade, thank you,” he said.

Joshua plopped himself down next to Brandon, sulking as he eyed his woman. Brandon could already tell he was trying to figure out how long he could last without the sex. Brandon knew it was not long. “What did they say about side-effects?”

Sarah shrugged. “Usual stuff, I think. Stuffy nose, mild fever, fatigue, and what not,” she replied.

“And I’m sure they have something for that too,” said Brandon, still observing his friends.

Josh narrowed his eyes. “It’s that what not shit that I am worried about,” he said.

Sarah sat down next to him and fixed him a hard, unforgiving stare. “Get the shot. Today. I don’t need two pussies in my life,” she replied.

Brandon pointed his fork at Sarah as he spoke to Josh. "You were wrong. *That* was cold," he offered.

"Fuck!" said Josh, pounding his head on the table. Brandon made him a plate. Pulling his head up, Brandon placed the plate before him and Josh started eating without missing a beat. "You know," he said between his sasquatch-sized bite. "I'm only doing this because I fucking love you."

Sarah smiled triumphantly as she accepted a plate from Brandon. "Say whatever you need to save face, lover. You aren't winning this one," she said before regarding Brandon. "So, what about you, Brandon? Are you going for the Omega Vaccine too?"

Brandon offered a polite smile as he shook his head. "I'm afraid not. I have to work today," he said.

"And after that?" she asked.

"Something else, I am sure," replied Brandon.

Josh exchanged a glance and a smile with Sarah before he responded. "Yeah, we thought that might be the case. God knows what will happen if you see any blood, especially yours," he said.

Brandon looked insulted. "That is untrue and unfair. You know damn well I hate the sight of all blood equally," he countered.

"Still though," said Sarah as she finally put her brush down. "These are strange times we find ourselves in, and I mean more than usual. It's better safe than sorry."

Brandon put down his fork. "Look, I will admit that things are pretty batshit out there. It seems like everyone is fixed on that Mayan calendar doomsday shit and using it as an excuse to go nuts. But I'm going to keep things normal, especially on the home front. If I must get that damn shot, I will. But first I am going to see what the hell it does to you two," he said.

Josh sneered sarcastically. "Well holy Van Dyke there, Dick, thanks a pant load," he offered.

Brandon smiled as he stood up to take his plate in to the sink. "All's fair in love and roommates," he offered cheerfully.

Sarah sighed. "Yeah, about that," she started.

At the sound of her voice, Brandon lowered his head and returned to the table. Crossing his arms and leaning on the counter, he prepared himself for what was next. "I think I know what this is about," he said shaking his head. "Again."

"Yeah," said Josh trailing off a second before continuing. "It's about your brother. Again. His presence is getting old. Again."

"Actually, it never stopped. Though I think it is getting worse," observed Sarah.

"Thank god it's only temporary," mused Brandon.

Josh slammed a fist on the table before looking apologetically at the décor. "It's been a fucking year, dude! Face it, your brother's a squatter and he's not going anywhere. Not unless it's by force or gunpoint."

Brandon rolled his eyes as he threw up his hands and slouched his shoulders. "Look, I'm trying, okay? I have been respecting your wishes. I have contained his slovenly ways to his room…mostly," he replied.

Joshua crossed his arms. "Dude. It's not just that. We could live with that. We've lived with that. But damn if he didn't have to endicken himself further and escalate," he said.

"Big time," mumbled Sarah as she bit down on a fork filled with eggs.

"Oh?" said Brandon.

"Yeah," said Josh. "You remember that birthday cake my mom made me? You know the one with the strawberry cream icing that would make any set of nipples hard at the taste?"

"Delicious stuff indeed," said Brandon in remembrance.

"Well forget about it, cause your bro ate the whole fucking thing himself while we were out," said Josh.

"As 'kindness' he left a bite and a fork on the plate in the fridge. Oh, yeah…that was before he went back and ate that too," said Josh.

"Oh shit," said Brandon.

"Yeah," said Josh. "And that's just the icing on the cake. Not the good icing I had been looking forward to for a whole god damn year, mind you. You know how he keeps his room just a sneeze and a fart shy of a pig pen?"

"Unfortunately so," said Brandon.

"Well we come home now, and he is snacking and watching shit in our room. We caught him yesterday half naked and eating Funyons," growled Josh.

"That is a relief, cause I'm sure he could have been worse about it," said Brandon.

"He forgot to mention he procured a pair of my panties as a napkin because the kitchen was too far away. Though he was sweet enough to say I smelled even better laced with Funyuns before he asked me to fetch him a soda," added Sarah.

"I stand corrected," said Brandon.

"We are planning on putting a padlock on our bedroom when we leave home now, B. I mean, what kind of shit is that?" asked Joshua.

"For him, normal," sighed Brandon.

Josh then pointed to the bathroom. "Poor Sarah walked in on him laid out, bare-assed in the tub. He had loofa in one hand and lubricant in the other, drunk out of his mind. I don't know what the fuck he was doing in there, but I don't want to feel dirty while I am trying to get clean in the shower, man," he said.

"I see your point," said Brandon.

"Are you sure?" Josh asked. "We got a list, man. And trust me, it's just getting started."

Brandon held up a hand to stop them. "No, I get it. I will talk to him tonight. He shapes up or he ships out. You have my word," he said before fetching his light jacket and heading to the door.

"You see that you do, B!" said Josh as Brandon departed. "Cause if he keeps fucking with my hair care products, I'm shoving my mousse so far up his ass I'll have to twist his god damn ears to use it. I have only not killed him yet cause he's your brother, man."

"Always a gentleman and a saint," said Brandon glumly from the door. "See you kids tonight. Good luck with the vaccine and try not to kill my brother until I get home," he said before he was gone.

The two lovers finished their plates in silence as they thought on the day's events. Finally, Joshua grinned at Sarah as an idea formed. "You know what would ease my mind about this whole shot thing right now? You and me. On the table. Right now," he said.

Sarah shook her head triumphantly as she took both their plates to the kitchen. "I told you, not until you get the shot," she said.

"Well you didn't rule out hands stuff or head!" he said before Sarah shook growled and returned to their bedroom. "Babe? Babe!" Defeated, Josh banged his head on the table, realizing that an errant piece of egg was now stuck to his forehead. "Fuck, I gotta do my hair again," he groaned before heading toward the bathroom.

Now free of the insanity at home, Brandon found himself in his car, enjoying those blissful, music-filled moments before work. Free of costumers, free of roommates, free of his brother, his commute was one of the highlights of his day. Hell, sometimes he would jump on errands or picking up things at the store just to get out of Dodge for a few glorious minutes. For Brandon, “me-time” was quality time.

And this blissful time died just about every time he pulled into the mall’s parking lot.

Cedar Park Mall was just about everything you could ask for in a mall. It had endured and evolved with the times and had everything you would want in a shopping experience. Brandon had in fact loved going to it as a kid. Yet something about it had changed since his youth, and the change irked him like a friend talking through a movie. At one point some years prior, Cedar Park had added a major retail store called Bordstrom, and that had been the pioneer beacon to the most elitist, pompous, and yuppie-esque patrons the city had to offer.

Eventually the mall began to cater to the higher class of costumer, metaphorically turning their nose at the regular everyday Joes and Janes. Prices went up. The regular crowd waned. Mom and pop stores faded from memory to be replaced with snootier and pricier versions. A few stores held out, and depending on the costumer, they were either an eyesore or the last bastions of goodness within the whole shopping outlet. These days there was little hope left, yet Brandon and the other holdouts held firmly to those hopes through the dark times.

Now parked, Brandon geared himself for battle. It was not so much of a life or death struggle, but rather a struggle to keep a smile, his kindness, and especially composure. To Brandon, “the costumer is always right” craze had devolved customers into people who needed to be right, or took out their hostilities on employees, or just wanted their asses wiped for them outright. It was a battle to stay ahead of the anger and no one was being paid nearly enough to endure such dumbassery.

There was just one more thing for Brandon to do in his pre-work ritual. With his radio turned up deeply, he gripped onto his door with his left hand and the passenger seat with his right. Lowering his head, he took a deep, calming breath. Holding it for long moments, he lifted his head toward the ceiling and expressed himself fully. "*Fuck*!!" It was a long and hearty culmination of release, preparation, and expression, screamed until he was practically blue. Thus complete, Brandon turned off his car and headed in to work.

Opening the doors, Brandon walked inside, immediately assaulted by the smell of leather and pompous indignation. It made his stomach curl and immediately he knew he would need more caffeine to endure the day. Walking swiftly to the food court, he targeted the little wannabe caffeine bistro of See Ya Latte. To Brandon the business was the bastard son of Starbucks, a dark infusion of poetry slam angst and corporate yuppie love. Their saving grace was the fact that some of their roasts were tasty, so long as the baristas didn't talk you into dolling them up too much.

Hitting the counter, a young man of no more than nineteen put on his best attempt at basking his nose in brown. "Good morning! And what shall you be partaking in today, good sir?" he inquired.

Brandon lifted his light jacket aside enough to show his nametag. "Cut the crap, Kevin. This isn't our first dance. Large Depth Charge, two extra shots of espresso," he said.

The young man named Kevin's eyes widened at the recognition. "Oh, it's you," he said as he looked nervously at the register. “You know, that is really a lot of caffeine,” he said.

Brandon placed his forearm on the counter as he leaned in on Kevin. “You’re frigging adorable, really. When it comes to caffeine, I know what I’m about. Just please make the drink. Further delay threatens your chances at a gratuity,” he offered before slapping a five on the counter.

Kevin then offered his smile again as he pushed his agenda. “Would you like to add-”

“-Sure wouldn’t, but thank you, Kevin,” said Brandon, declining the frou-frou upcharges.

As Kevin set to work, Brandon turned and leaned his back on the counter as he looked over the food court. He could remember it vividly from his youth. So many of the delicious mainstays were gone, replaced by uppity chains. Upon Bordstrom’s arrival, the assault on the food court was next. Rent was raised, the locals couldn’t keep up for long, and thus the mall’s journey toward the Darkside was complete.

“Here you are, sir,” said Kevin, placing the piping hot black elixir upon the counter for Brandon.

Brandon nodded as he placed a few dollars in the tip jar. “You have my thanks, Kevin,” he said as he started to walk away.

“You keep drinking that much caffeine and it will be the end of you,” offered Kevin politely.

“Then I will see you in hell!” replied Brandon over his shoulder, realizing immediately Han Solo had done it better in Empire.

Sipping the piping hot black goodness in his cup, Brandon ventured over to the corner of the food court. A slow smile crept over his face, for he saw the head custodian Cliff Tomlinson watching the court with stern care. With his back to the wall, Cliff held his mop in both hands as he stared over his long beard. Cliff was one of the good ones that had endured the changes of the mall and Brandon was damn glad the man was still around.

As Brandon stood next to him, Cliff acknowledged him without taking his eyes off the court. "Hello, Brandon," he said before smelling the air. "Depth-Charge, extra espresso. Expecting one of those nights already, I see," he said.

"That's what I love about you, Cliff. You get me," said Brandon, taking another drink. "I have one of those gut feelings, like something's in the air. I just can't decide if it's bad luck or if fate is out to fuck me over."

Cliff eyed Brandon for a second. Somehow the man's gritty brown beard and vibrant eyes made him a mix between a loving Santa and a pissed-off Viking. "You've grown a bit cynical, Brandon, but I get it. Something is indeed in the air," said Cliff as he looked about. "I don't know if it's a full moon or downright fuckery afoot, but I feel it too."

"Glad I am not the only one. I don't know what retrograde has to do with it, but Mercury can fuck all the way off when it's in it," said Brandon, relishing another drink before continuing. "And what are you doing over here? Looking for the future Mrs. Tomlinson?"

Cliff chuckled faintly. "Not at all. Just keeping tabs on my mall. There's a guy in Topic of the Town. He smells like a shoplifter," said Cliff without turning his head toward the mentioned store. "I am just here to make sure he doesn't try to escape the food court exit if he does."

Brandon smiled at him. "Custodian. Guardian. Friend. Is there anything this man can't do?" he offered. Cliff always came off as a sage-like father figure and had made Brandon feel welcomed from day one.

"I am sure there's something," said Cliff.

Just then, another voice filled the food court. "Ya'll just gonna leave your trays on the table like you brought your butlers with you? Not how it works here, folks. Yeah, I'm calling ya'll out. Get back over here and clean up after yourselves!"

Brandon and Cliff turned their heads to see another custodian with his dry mop pointing at a group who had just finished eating. The sharp-dressed party of five looked about the food court to see all eyes were now on them. Indignantly they returned to the table to claim their trays, staring daggers at the custodian as they did. Still holding their tray, one of the patrons, a middle-aged woman, stood angrily in front of the custodian.

"It's a shame when life doesn't teach a man to know his place in the order of things," she said to him.

The custodian was unmoved. "Well it's an even bigger damn shame when someone thinks money and position excuse them from being a decent human being," he said.

"Heathen," spat the woman as she stormed off at the perceived insubordination.

The custodian reached for the table and held up the salt shaker that was left behind. "Don't you worry none, mam. I'll take care of this, cause you are obviously salty enough as is, ya half-chewed heifer!"

Cliff shook his head as some of the crowd either gasped or applauded, looking somehow pleased and displeased at the same time. "God damnit, Ron," he said to himself before looking at Brandon. "I am going to hear about that one later," he added.

"Well if you need another witness on his behalf, let me know," replied Brandon. "I know we pay for it in the end, but it is always good to see justice served."

“Yeah,” said Cliff, crossing his arms and hugging his mop. “But it’s getting harder and harder to defend my crew. If we didn’t keep this mall running as well as we do, the owner would have replaced us for new blood long ago.”

“Thank god you are indispensable,” said Brandon as Ron saw them and approached, waving.

Approaching them with an infectious grin, Ron Stohlman approached them. He was affectionately called Panda, though most people couldn’t remember why. Ron kept his balding hair trimmed short and wore a goatee long enough to be dragged around by it. Adjusting his glasses, Ron slid next to Brandon as the two exchanged a fist bump.

“How goes it, Panda?” asked Brandon.

“Oh, living a blessed life here, brother, that’s for sure. It’s always a great day when I can put a bunch of assholes on blast. How about yourself?” Brandon held up his Depth Charge silently. “Ah, that good, huh?”

“Pretty much,” said Brandon.

“You know, we are going to hear about that, Ron,” said Cliff.

Ron nodded. “I’m sure we are, bossman. But someone had to say something about that shit.”

To this, Cliff nodded. “Carry on, soldier,” said Cliff.

Ron gave him a quick salute. “You got it,” said Ron as started to work on the floor with his dry mop.

“I still can’t believe he was actually in the military,” said Brandon. “He’s just so, carefree.”

Cliff nodded. “But still the kind of guy you want on your side in a scrap. It was probably that time that really taught him to grab life by the horns,” he said.

“A fair point,” said Brandon as he tried to take another sip of his coffee. Just then, the alarm at Topic of the Town went off. Brandon shook his head. “You called it, Cliff.”

"Yup," said Cliff as he procured his walkie-talkie. "Theft in progress. Shoplifter at Topic of the Town," he said before calling out to his co-worker. "Ron, attack pattern beta," he added. Ron simply nodded and positioned himself with his back to Topic of the Town, still mopping at the floor.

Brandon watched as a man holding stolen shirts came running toward the food court. His eyes were frantic, a definite combination of fear and the realization that he just done fucked up for the price of a few clothing garments. The taste in his acquisitions coupled with his present attire indicated he was good at making poor life choices. The employee at the Topic of the Town yelled at him as he streaked through the mall, knocking customers out of the way as he did so.

Nearing the food court, the man prepared to pass by Brandon and Cliff. Brandon kept drinking his coffee as Cliff swiftly ran his wet mop across the floor and back again. The thief hit the wet spot and started to slip, the merchandise in his hands now flying. As he stumbled forward surprised, Ron lifted his dry mop quickly, holding it out like a vengeful limbo bar. The man's face struck it solidly before he was lifted feet first off of the ground, landing on his back unconscious. Ron went back to mopping as he whistled a happy tune.

Brandon continued to watch as two more custodians emerged and entered the food court. Michael and Dennis quickly walked over to the unconscious man, picking up the stolen items before grabbing him up by the arms and legs as they hauled him off to the security office. As they passed by, Brandon gave them a nod as Cliff picked up the merchandise from the sleeping man's stomach. The lady from the Topic of the Town store thanked Cliff as he handed her the items. Cliff silently nodded before relaxing upon the wall again.

"You fuckers are a well-oiled machine," observed Brandon as he sipped his beverage once again. "Just remember when you officially run this place, I loved you before you were famous."

"Noted," said Cliff as he watched the security officer lumber over. The man huffed and wheezed, looking every bit of 300 pounds as he stopped next to Cliff and caught his breath.

"Where's the perp," gasped the man between breaths.

"It's been handled, no thanks to you," said Cliff. "He's already on his way to your office."

Still catching his breath, the security officer balled his fists on his hips. "We've talked about this before, Cliff. You clean the floors and I handle the crime," he said.

Cliff continued watching the food court as he responded to the man. "Glen, the day you can handle more than a sandwich is the day I will happily use my mop for just cleaning. Now please fuck off," he said.

Glen stifled several obscenities that longed to pour from his lips. His hand went to the taser on his belt but thought better of it. Shaking his head, the large security man turned and headed to his office at a much slower pace than he had arrived. Cliff watched him depart in disgust.

"Must be nice being the mall owner's cousin," said Cliff.

"Neither one of them ever miss a chance to rub it in our faces, or a meal for that matter," mused Brandon.

Cliff looked at his watch. "Well it looks like you better get to work, Brandon," he said.

Brandon looked at his phone. "Shit, you're right," he said, giving Cliff a slap on his arm. "Thanks for having my back, Cliff. I'll catch you in a bit."

"Anytime, my friend," said Cliff with a faint smile. He then returned to his vigil over the food court. "And don't forget to love your job and what you do," he added.

Brandon looked about as he raised his cup over his head in salute. "It's not the job I hate, my friend!" he said before he was off and away.

Brandon kept his tunnel vision and primary focus on his coffee as he walked, making sure his nametag was covered. Just working at the mall prompted incessant questions, even if they were about places that you didn't work. Brandon simply wanted to sip his delicious beverage and be left the hell alone for as long as allowed.

At last and with reserved reluctance, Brandon made it to his job. Taking a moment to finish his coffee, he smiled at the wonderful sight. Dabbles and Dorkery stood before him in its full, geeky splendor. Dabbles and Dorkery was in fact a nerd emporium hopelessly devoted to all things nerdy. Brandon had loved the place so god damn much he had to work there and help ensure its continuing survival.

Adorned with stand-up posters of superheroes, the emporium shimmered with inviting, luminous décor as if a large titan or god had eaten a cache of multiple fandoms and shit them out into one glorious store. Dabbles and Dorkery held comics, books, tabletop games, video games, card games, dice, movies, toys, props, costumes and collectibles. The owner often claimed it was enough to make Stan Lee masterfully splooge while screaming "Excelsior!"

Brandon walked into the organized chaos, happy that the store was full of his kind of people for the moment. It was as it should be: a group was in the corner playing out a session of Dungeons and Dragons. Awesomely epic fantasy scores were playing over the speakers. Patrons were exploring the fare with child-like glee. A kid was discussing with the owner how to modify his recently purchased costume for the upcoming Comicon. Two grown ass men were about to duel with lightsabers for the sheer hell of it.

Yeah, this part Brandon fucking loved.

Going around the counter, Brandon removed his jacket and clocked in. Discarding his empty coffee cup, he walked back up front ready for fun and war. The boss said goodbye to the young man who happily left the store with his purchase before approaching Brandon. He gave his employee a nod and a smile as he approached.

Brandon tried to gauge what his day would be like based on his boss's mood. Jim Martin was a nerd at heart, tried and true. With his build and trimmed, graying facial hair he could pass in the normal crowds any time, but Jim was in love with the nerd life. He made his own costumes and put his heart and soul into his store. Brandon had met him when he was but a simple customer and was won over eventually to be a part of the team.

"Thank god you're here," said Brandon's boss. "The sharks have been circling," he said.

"Yay," said Brandon lifelessly. "Hello, misery. I bet you are quite happy to have some company."

Jim nodded as he surveyed his store. "You bet I am. I mean I am happy Jay's here too, but three heads are better than two. And I rather be prepared and mitigate any abuse laid upon us."

Brandon nodded. "Fair enough. Me and Jay will tank'em and you spank'em. I'll hop to it," he said before going around the counter to help customers.

Brandon patrolled the aisles, helping where he could and answering questions when needed. Jay Sayers, a long haired, soft featured beauty of a man gave Brandon a smile, happy to see him at work. Brandon then continued his rounds, straightening up and organizing when it was needed.

And then, it happened.

“Excuse me. Sir? Sir!”

“Fuck, that didn’t take long at all,” mumbled Brandon before he strapped on a smile like a gallant dildo and turned to face his newest customer. He could already feel the darkness descending, even before he turned.

Brandon's worse fears were confirmed, for he came face to face with an obviously uppity customer. The man wore a white button up shirt and a brown suit jacket over it. Below this he was squeezed into tight pants and tan, fancy loafers without socks. From his brown-rimmed glasses, the carefully styled blonde looked upon Brandon as if he were nothing. The man looked severely out of place within Dabbles and Dorkery and anxious to be free of the place.

Brandon fought tooth and nail to keep the smile spackled to his face. "How can I help you today, sir?" he asked through almost clenched teeth.

The man looked over Brandon completely before sighing discontentedly. "Well I suppose you will do," he said as he looked about the store. Brandon surmised he had a BMW in the lot either taking two spaces or in the handicapped spot. "I am looking for something for my nephew's birthday. What do you have?"

Brandon almost didn't know how to answer such a question as he looked about the heavily adorned nerd store. "A little bit of everything actually. What does he like?"

The man shrugged indifferently as if such knowledge was of no importance. "How would I know? Though I am told he is into Star Wars and such," he said, like bile was touching his tongue.

Brandon smiled. "Well, that's a good start," he offered before he pointed toward the other end of the store. "If you follow me, I will show you what we have in that department."

Brandon led the man over, who looked annoyed just having to walk further into the store. He kept a distance from the patrons and the shelves as if he were avoiding the plague. It was clear that even though Brandon and the man both spoke English, it would be impossible for them to speak the same language. Brandon prayed this would be a quick sell, and further cursed himself for holding hopes he knew were vain.

Coming to the appropriately Star Wars themed section, Brandon pointed at it proudly. "As you can see, we have a wonderful array of Star Wars fare for any ardent fan," said Brandon.

"My god," said the man in completely amazement. "People actually buy this sort of thing?"

Brandon clenched his fists momentarily before continuing "Most definitely. Jim hasn't remained a fixture in this mall for over 20 years with wishes and happy thoughts," he offered, eliciting no laugh from the man. Not that he expected one. This man was obviously so self-absorbed he would fuck himself if given the chance.

The man looked upon the shelves at the toys, action figures and books. "Hmm, this is all foreign to me. Though I do believe he said something about loving a Millennial Eagle of some sort?"

Brandon twitched, fighting back the aneurysm that was attempting to end his misery. "Sir, I wholeheartedly think you mean the *Millennium Falcon*, one of the most iconic ships in science fiction," he stammered before pointing to a box containing a full replica of awesomeness.

The man looked at the price immediately and scoffed at it. "Maybe I can just get something close to it," he mused before pointing at another ship. "What about that one? Is it cheaper?"

Brandon looked painfully in the direction the man was pointing, cringing once more. "Sir, while that is an awesome ship in its own right, that is the *Serenity*, a firefly-class ship from a whole different story that your nephew might still be too young to know. But it’s an awesome series if you ever want to watch it one day," said Brandon, suddenly wanting to feed the yuppie to a band of Reavers hopped up on steroids and viagra.

"I doubt it," said the man as he pointed to another beloved character, standing stoically while holding his trademark weapon. "What's Sasquatch doing in this section, and why is he armed?"

Brandon looked over the man's shoulder, his eyes widening with horror and disgust. "That's Chewbacca from Star Wars. He's a Wookie. And if he were here right now and heard you call him that he would have likely torn your arms off," said Brandon.

The man looked at Brandon dubiously. "You do know he doesn't exist, right?" he asked.

Finally, Brandon lowered his head in defeat before pointing to the door. "Get out," he said.

"Excuse me?" asked the man.

"You heard me loud and clear, sir. For my sake and yours, please get the hell out. You are way out of place here. Don't disappoint your nephew. Get him a gift card. Let him get what he wants joyfully because you are going to fail miserably," said Brandon.

Color rushed to the man's face. "Well I never," he huffed.

"I doubt that," said Brandon. "And if you return here you will again most likely."

The man threw up his nose. "Do you have a manager I can speak to about your behavior?"

Brandon smiled as he pointed to the counter. "That's Jim at the counter. Tell him about Sasquatch. Trust me, that will clear everything up quite quick like," he said.

"I'll have your job for this," said the man.

"You wouldn't know what to do with it," said Brandon.

As the man stormed up to the counter, Brandon turned, fighting the urge to apologize to all Star Wars and Firefly fans worldwide. He could hear faintly the man talking to Jim at the counter. Brandon waited patiently then for the payoff, for it was coming soon enough. And he was surely not disappointed as he heard a fist slam on the counter.

"Get the hell out of my store!" raged Jim as he pointed to the door. "Walk your ass out or I'll throw it out myself!"

As Jim came around the counter, it squashed any other protests from the man. The haughty yuppie turned tail and fled. Jim followed him to the end of his shop before he settled himself and return to the counter. Brandon smiled and returned to work. It was nice knowing his boss had his back.

"Brandon, could you watch the counter a spell? I need a moment. And lunch," said Jim from across the store.

"Sure thing, boss," said Brandon as he made his way to the front.

Setting his hands upon the counter, Brandon surveyed the store again as Jim departed. There were more of what he would call their people in the store than not, but his recent encounter with the yuppie dickhead had left him more than annoyed.

Brandon then had the pleasure of ringing up an avid comic collector for new issues before he was faced with another one of "them." A stern, evaluating woman approached him with a large item, obviously annoyed she had to wait her turn. She wore a black designer dress and carefully crafted frosted hair that simply screamed “Fuck you, I’m better than you are.” And as she waited for Brandon, she offered him a fake smile with unusually white teeth.

“Find everything you need, mam?” Brandon asked as he scanned the boxed toy.

“Oh, yes thank you,” said the woman matter of factly. “My son just loves the Power Rangers. He’s going to flip when he sees this.”

Brandon halted the transaction, holding the box face up and showing it to the woman. “Mam, I don’t want to be a stickler to detail, but you should know that this is a Voltron, Defender of the Universe set. Similar principles except Voltron came first, was ultimately better, was horribly copied and didn’t have live action teens prancing about in overactive martial art poses. For your child’s sake, it is important you know the difference.”

“They look the same to me,” said the woman, obviously offended.

“Perhaps, yes,” said Brandon patiently. “But when your kiddo finds out they are not you will just be back up here returning it and likely pissed at me for not doing my job.”

“I think you are just trying to get more money from me,” said the woman.

Brandon shook his head. “No. Actually I want you to go with the wrong toy only so you can return and we can have these moments,” said Brandon as he rung her up.

The woman swiped her card and completed her transaction before she snatched the bag out of Brandon’s hand. “Like I will ever want to shop here again,” she spat before storming out of the store.

Brandon called out to her. “Oh, miss! Just remember, store policy frowns on concealed weapons, so when you return please make sure to remove the stick up your ass," said Brandon with good cheer. "And bring a receipt to expedite the "I-fucking-told-you-so process. And have a nice day!" Brandon then laid his elbows upon the counter and buried his face in his hands. "This can't get any worse," he breathed.

And he was fucking wrong.

Just then, Brandon was dismayed to hear the painful sound of M&Ms cascading from their container to overflow the receptacle and spill upon the floor. There holding the level was a young teen looking equally guilty and busted. Jim kept candy dispensers for the gamers that came in and charged by the bag size you filled. He also had a sign that said it was five bucks if you pulled a lever without a bag underneath it.

Jay pointed to the guilty teen, raising his voice. "That's five bucks, buddy. You can pay Brandon up at the counter," he said.

Just then, an adult near Jay placed his hands at his hips and puffed out his chest. "I need to see a manager at once," he demanded.

Jay pointed to Brandon as he fetched the broom and dustpan. Jim's not here. You will have to talk to our second-in-command," said Jay, shaking his head, obviously knowing where this was going.

The man, adorned in a black jacket that went past his knees over a casual suit, stormed up to Brandon. He gave Brandon a hard stare as he looked over his shoulder at the guilty party, obviously his son, and then to an equally snooty woman, obviously his wife. He waited expectantly for the respect his gaze said he so rightly deserved. Brandon prepared for war.

"Would that be cash or charge?" asked Brandon.

The man placed a hand on the counter as he tried to intimidate Brandon. "Well I personally think if we are paying five dollars, we should get some candy to go with it. My son obviously didn't see the sign, so I refuse to pay for what was an honest mistake. Wouldn't you agree?" spouted the man.

Brandon shook his head coolly. "No, I wouldn't actually," he replied.

"Excuse you?" said the man.

"No, cause there is no excuse for this," said Brandon as he pointed to the man in his family. "We put that sign up so parents would watch after their kiddos under five. And here you are defending your boy who is obviously thirteen or fourteen and of a damn age he should know better and who can in fact read. And the sad part is you don't even see that you aren't doing him any favors by getting him out of trouble," he said before taking a moment to look at the man's son. "Use your head next time, buddy. Your daddy won't be around to save you all the time. You are partially to blame for being douchey, but he is to blame too for enabling you."

"I don't think I like your tone, sir. And I am the costumer here, so I am in the right."

"Wrong," said Brandon.

"It's true!"

"It's not," replied Brandon.

"We don't owe you anything."

"Wrong again," answered Brandon.

"I have half a mind to reach over that counter and teach you a lesson you will never forget."

Brandon sighed. "Well you were right about the half mind part for sure, but you know what?" Brandon held out his hands, obviously casting his last fucks into the wind. "I am done with you. This is one of the few times a blood phobia comes in handy," he answered, grabbing the box cutter next to the register.

Deploying the blade, Brandon made a little stab on his left

palm. Grimacing, he put the cutter down while clenching his injured hand. Smiling, he raised his left, giving the man the bird as he saw a bit of blood trickle down his wrist. And at this, Brandon passed the fuck out right there behind the counter, taking his first, unofficial break for the day.

3

THE BROTHER, OH BROTHER

Aaron Thomas Morgan drifted blissfully through la-la land, fervently oblivious to the outside world. Resting upon his stomach, his mouth wailed like a congested basset hound as he slept. A fan set to high sat inches from his face, and by the periodic thrusts he offered his bed he was having a good dream. Aaron was fully immersed in his reverie, save for the annoyance of a blaring distraction.

Just as Aaron was about to administer sweet lovins' fully, he found himself dragged out of slumber like a wounded soldier from a firefight. Through a foggy haze he moaned, a sound made sillier by the close proximity to the fan. Confused and disoriented, he searched about dully for the sound, realizing that was not his alarm, nor his back up alarm. It was Brandon's "oh shit, you're really fucking late, dumbass" alarm.

Aaron searched about with his hands, hoping the focus would make his schlong take the hint and redistribute the blood to the rest of his body. Under his pillow he found his first alarm. Apparently in his sleep he had unplugged and hogtied it with its own cord. The second took more time, for it was lying in a broken heap across the room, having been thrown and smashed against the wall. Groaning again, he turned off Brandon's failsafe and rose at long last.

Stretching as he fought off the effects of his waning wang, Aaron emitted a simultaneous fart and yawn as he scratched himself. Inwardly he laughed at all the fuckers that said he couldn't multitask. He then looked about his room, a not so careful product of complete, utter, and shockingly horrible neglect. Traversing it was not a task for the faint-hearted.

Before Aaron's two stained mattresses resting on the floor resided a landmine of trash, dirty clothes, filthy plates, and cups that still held liquid in them. Looking for a useable undershirt, Aaron discovered a half-consumed glass of milk that has curdled enough to be able to possibly jump up and latch to his face. Crooked and tattered posters of jibes, quips, and dead musicians were strewn across the wall. Sitting upon an old milk crate was a paused PlayStation 2, its games stacked in a pile outside their cases collecting dust and scratches.

Some people called him a slob, not realizing the dedication it took to achieve the kind of reckless abandon that he could.

Tiptoeing through his room, Aaron cussed as his foot stepped on a plate and the remnants of a meal he had four days ago. Wiping his foot on a stolen pair of Sarah's panties, Aaron smelled the undies, smiled, and exited his room as he tossed the underwear toward his bed. Sadly, it landed in the curdling milk glass and would be the last anyone ever saw of them.

Now in the bathroom, Aaron examined himself in the mirror, running a hand over the stubble on his chin. A handsome man, Aaron was not below using his looks and charms to get his way. Unfortunately, even such looks and charisma went only so far, for he could tell his welcome was waning with his brother and roommates. Procuring Josh's toothbrush and Sarah's toothpaste, he contemplated his dilemma as he brushed his teeth.

Aaron then used some hand sanitizer wipes to clean his armpits and crotch. He wasn't even going to try a shower. If Josh beat him to it then there would likely be no hot water till the evening. He proceeded to gargle with his brother's mouthwash, reminding himself to remind Brandon he needed to get more soon.

Heading into his brother's room, Aaron procured fresh socks, pants, and underwear before discarding his old pair of boxers on Brandon's floor. Dressed, he used his brother's deodorant and cologne before checking himself out in the mirror with a wink. Looking at the time, he realized he was running way late and goaded himself to move more slowly. Fashionably late was part of his charm, especially when it came to work. Aaron liked to think he was swooping in to save the day.

Aaron was generally wrong in this assumption but try telling him that.

Heading through the living room and into the kitchen, Aaron opened the door to the fridge, whistling a happy tune. He then grimaced, for pickings were slim. His brother and roommates needed to stock up again soon. Aaron then set his eyes on Brandon's leftovers from the previous night. Snatching up the combination Lo Mein, he procured a fork and paced the living room as he ate on the fly.

Aaron then heard a door open along with a hopeful voice. "I think he's gone, thank god," said Sarah.

Josh exited their room before catching sight of Aaron in the living room. “Nope. Here he is, babe,” he said. Sarah sighed angrily, well fucking beyond the days of hiding such resentment.

“Sup, guys,” said Aaron through bites. One of the noodles fell on the carpet. He scooped it up and tossed it toward the kitchen sink, missing as it struck and stuck upon the cabinet.

“Morning, man,” said Josh darkly as he watched Aaron devour the contents of Brandon’s leftovers. “Good to see you so chipper while you show your brotherly fucking love.”

“He wouldn’t want me to go hungry,” said Aaron as he pointed toward the fridge. “Which reminds me, there might be a necessary grocery run in your near future.”

Josh crossed his arms, resisting the ever-loving urge to punch the ever-loving shit out of Aaron. "You’re right. Are you chipping in this time, man? Cause the groceries would make it a lot fucking longer if you did," he said.

Aaron grimaced. "Money's a little tight this week, with all those expenses that came up unexpectantly."

Sarah could no long hold her tongue. "You mean the sale at Game Stop?"

"That's the one," said Aaron, smiling at her. "I mean, what can ya do, right?"

"You fucking buy groceries and pay bills first," growled Josh. "I am getting damn tired of having to label the food, cause even that is not working anymore."

Aaron shook his head. "Untrue," he offered as he pointed to the crotch of his pants. There resting were two of Josh's stickers put together that read Mine. Not yours. "Now that message is solely for you, Josh," he said before winking at Sarah.

"Oh, that's fucking it," said Josh as he went to unleash the wrath of god upon Aaron. Sarah stepped between them, holding Josh back.

"Nope," said Sarah. "Not in the house. No blood on the carpet. Stay cool for Brandon's sake."

Josh threw his hands up, flipping off a god who obviously loved dicking with him. "Babe, I have been playing it cool. I have been so god damn cool about this that I almost didn't recognize myself in the mirror today," he said before pointing at Aaron. "But this motherfucker keeps walking all over that fucking cool that I think we're about two weeks away from him tea-bagging it for shits and giggles, or us in our sleep."

"Damn," said Aaron as he took another bite of noodles. "I knew from the sounds coming from your room that you two were into some kinky shit, but damn."

Josh's eyes widened. "You want kinky? Wait till you see where this foot is gonna go," he offered.

"We haven't time for this," said Sarah as she went and fetched her purse. "We're off to get our vaccine shot," she said before stopping to sneeze. "Before it's too late."

"Bless you," said Aaron as he reached in his back pocket, handing her a silky, clean handkerchief.

"Thank you," said Sarah, surprised as she accepted the cloth. She went to blow her nose before she realized that he had, in fact, handed her a pair of her panties. "Oh, you sick fuck."

"Oops," said Aaron.

"Motherfucker," said Josh as he stepped toward Aaron again.

Sarah held a finger up to stop him before slapping Aaron on the back of his head. "Again, we don't have the time. Let's go, Josh," she said as she headed for the door.

Josh walked by Aaron in very close proximity. Aaron held up a noodle laden fork and offered him a bite. "Just wait till we all get home tonight. We are going to have a real 'come to Jesus' talk with you and Brandon.

"Kinky," said Aaron as he put the container carelessly on the counter. "So, you guys are heading out, huh?"

"Obviously," said Josh as he made it to the door with Sarah.

"So, you mind giving me a ride then to work?"

"Motherfucker!" spat Josh, banging his head against the nearest wall.

The ride to the mall was…awkward to say the least. Sarah said nothing as Josh merely mumbled and cussed to himself as he strangled the steering wheel. Aaron sat casually in the back, searching about for opportunity. Sarah had made the horrible mistake of leaving her purse in the back seat. Unbeknownst to her, she was 20 bucks lighter than she started out with.

Pulling into the mall parking lot, Josh was nice enough to almost stop his car completely to let Aaron out. Aaron, grateful for the ride, let one rip before he jumped from the car and slammed the door shut. As Josh fought to roll down the window to claim fresh air and shout out a fresh batch of obscenities, Aaron walked inside victoriously and headed to the food court.

With every step toward his job, Aaron's features grew grimmer. His demeanor changed fully as he assumed his game face. This wasn't work. This was a battle. And as soon as he clocked in it was Mortal Fucking Kombat, baby.

Aaron set his sights on Roberto's Italian Deli, a locally owned eatery that had been talked into coming to the mall some years back. Selling hot and cold subs and pizza whole or by the slice, Roberto's was a staple in the mall. With its food, the deli could cater to a wide range of clienteles, which had aided in its survival during the mall's "conversion." Of course, it didn't hurt that their food was fucking delicious to boot.

Aaron had been hired at Roberto's at 16 as a part time job during school. Years later, he was the place's premiere pizza guy, having honed the recipes into an artful craft. It had made him invaluable, indispensable, and also even more of a pain in the ass to the owner. It was a fact that Aaron had used to his fullest advantage.

Entering the employee door, Aaron clocked in and donned his apron. As he did, a fellow employee offered him a small cup filled with equal parts Mountain Dew and energy shot. The two of them slammed the contents of their drinks and slapped each other in the face before Aaron nodded his thanks and set to work. Grabbing a ball of pizza dough, Aaron began to exert his magic as he looked over the incoming orders.

Coming from the back office, Aaron's boss balled his two large hands on his hips. Bob, the owner of the store looked like a big bellied New Yorker trying to pass as a young urban professional. He wore the khakis and button up shirt, but looked like a fish out of water in them. It was obvious the lunch rush had put him on edge and orders were backing up. Aaron knew he was there but paid him no mind.

"You're late," said Bob.

"But just in time to save the day," said Aaron absently. The employee from before came up front and placed a baseball cap backwards on Aaron's head. "Thanks, David," he added.

Bob shook his head angrily. "I am about sick of this crap. You show up when you are supposed to or you're outta here," he said.

Aaron stopped and gave him a stern look. "I could leave right now if you want. I bet half the crew goes with me and you will get to do the lunch rush yourself," he countered.

Bob threw up his hands, shaking his head and muttering to himself as he went back to his office. Satisfied he was left to his own devices, Aaron smiled and got down to business. Food was an art and it showed in his efforts. He was shit at a lot of things, including being a human being most times, but Aaron never shirked the food he made. Within moments he had fashioned a god damn gorgeous pizza before tossing it in the oven.

It was then that his fellow employee and pizza maker leaned over to him. The employee was a serious looking man of Mexican ancestry. He looked overly confident, adorned with stern eyes and a trimmed goatee. "Hey man," he said as he topped slices of pizza to go into the oven.

"What's up, David?" asked Aaron.

"It is David," said David.

"That's what I said and that's what I always say," said Aaron.

"No. Da-veed."

"Yeah, David," said Aaron.

"Da-veed."

"Da-veed or David, however you say it is still David, Da-veed," said Aaron.

"But it is Da-veed. That is how you say it," said David.

Aaron shook his head. "Yeah, man. I fucking get it. I do. But here in the states you better be prepared to be called both, cause it is gonna happen and you can't be getting pissed off at every person that calls you plain ol' David."

"Da-veed sounds better. The mamacitas like it better. It is the true name of a much-lover."

Aaron shook his head, grinning as he made another pizza. "God damn, I love your grasp of the English language," he offered as he continued his work. "But also, I am not a mamacita, man, so I am impervious to your much-loving ways."

"But still, man," David said.

Aaron threw another pizza in before looking at his coworker. "Let's talk about this after we take out this rush, or maybe over Coronas later. Deal?"

David smiled, giving Aaron a fist bump. "You got it," he said as they both began working like a well-oiled machine to bust through the growing line.

The two comrades proceeded to kick thorough ass, catching up orders on the pizza side. Their efficiency even gave David the time to flirt with some women as they picked up their pizza. Sometimes Aaron would have to remind him that they were in fact working still. These interruptions were often met with narrow-eyed scowls from David.

"Sorry to burst your bubble there, Senior Suave. Or was it El Guapo?"

"Callate, whetto," replied David jokingly.

The two friends continued their barbs at one another as an older woman grew annoyed by it. Stepping forward she put her ticket on the counter. "Excuse me, is my order ready yet?" she asked, most snarky like.

David approached her and picked up the ticket. Before looking at Aaron. "Hey, man. It says number 239," he said.

Aaron looked at the ticket order for 239. "Ah yes, mam. 239, a whole pizza, ordered three minutes ago. I promise it's in the hands of the oven now and not us. I am sorry if our attempts at levity are annoying you," he said.

"So, it's not ready yet," said the lady still being rude.

“Obviously,” said Aaron before he turned his back on her and checked the pizzas in the oven. “But we will call your number when it is. It will sound like 239.”

The woman crossed her arms and got further huffy about it. “I just want my pizza,” she said, most matter of factly.

“I wouldn’t advise it right now,” said Aaron. “The laws of time and reality apply to all of us, regardless of our perceived status.”

“I want my pizza now,” said the woman.

Aaron shrugged. “Fine, then.” He then proceeded to remove the half-cooked pizza from the oven, place it in a box, and close the box before handing it to the woman. “Order 239!” he yelled before returning to his work.

The woman opened the box and looked like she had been stabbed in the back. “Why, this isn’t even cooked properly!” she spat.

Aaron turned back around, handing another customer their cooked pizza as he stared angrily at her. “Oh, you think?” he said before leaning in closer. “Look, mam. I know we might be grating back here, but we know what the hell we’re doing. Please let me do my job and I will have you the best damn pizza in the city. But you are going to have to wait for it. If you want to step out and sit down, I’ll have David bring it to you.”

“Da-veed,” emphasized David.

“Shut it,” he told his friend before focusing again on the costumer. “But please for the love of baby Jesus, let us do what we do best. I’ll even throw in a brownie for yelling at you.”

“Fine,” said the woman as she made her way to the food court seating.

Satisfied, Aaron returned to his work, placing the half-finished pizza back in the oven and continuing to do what he did best. Most of those in earshot of the encounter with the woman left Aaron the hell alone then, a fact that pleased him greatly. He lost himself in his job, making pizza after pizza like works of delicious art. He and David even put on a little show with their dough-flinging abilities.

As the lunch rush began to die down and Aaron could see light at the end of the tunnel, Janette called out to him. “Hey, Aaron, this guy wants to know if you could make a special order,” she called out from the register.

“Fuck,” mumbled Aaron as he made his way to the register, still working a ball of pizza dough. “David, watch the oven.” And yes, he pronounced it Da-veed that time.

Walking to Janette, Aaron looked upon the special requester. He was a good-looking, sharp dressed man of his early twenties, appearing to Aaron as someone who had never been told no a day in his life. He was smiling, but Aaron saw through that fake-ass façade faster than Obi-Wan could lop off a hand in a cantina, which was pretty damn fast.

“What can I do for you, boss?” Aaron asked.

The man dove right in to his request. “Well, there is this place back in Chicago where I’m from that does this excellent deep-dish pizza that I absolutely love. I was wondering if I told you about it or showed you a pic if you could pull it off for me,” he said.

“Nope,” said Aaron immediately as he went to return to the oven.

“Wait, sir, you didn’t even hear my request out,” said the man.

Aaron paused, drew a long breath before turning to address the man. “Look, man, it doesn’t matter what request you have to make. You want something that isn’t on our menu. Now if you had some allergy or something, I would be glad to help, but you just want something you can’t have. I mean, you don't go into McDonald's and say, I want a Big-Mac but I want you to make it like a Whopper. Regardless, even if I made it and even if it fucking tasted good you would bitch about it to your friends saying how Roberto's isn't good and you haven't even tried one of our menu items. So again, nope. Sorry if this burns your ass. I suggest you pick something off the menu," he said.

"But," started the man.

"Or fuck all the way off back to Chicago and let them deal with you. You're holding up the line now," said Aaron.

"I will be heard!" snapped the man.

Aaron exchanged a glance with Janette before he took the sufficiently stretched pizza dough and put it over the man's head. "Loud and clear, asshole," said Aaron as he returned to his station. And while it wasn't a majority, many customers clapped as the dough laden man stormed out of the deli.

Returning to his work, Aaron felt a strange wave of peace wash over him as he set back to his duties. He spoke his peace. His regulars were fed, and all was well in his eyes. Aaron didn't consider himself a defender of justice, but he felt he had administered some today.

"Aaron!" yelled his boss. "My office! Now!"

Aaron grabbed a paper plate and put on a slice for himself as he gave a thumbs up to David. "Hold the fort again. I'll be back I suppose," he said before saluting with the slice and taking a bite as he headed to the office.

Inside the cramped office, Aaron sat eating his pizza contentedly as Bob tried to tear him a new one with his words. The vein on Bob's head popped out like an attention whore as the owner's face reddened with his fury. Aaron sat at an angle, careful not to let any of Bob's spittle land on his slice as he absorbed the brunt of the tirade. The nonchalance he displayed merely pushed Bob to the next level of pissedivity.

"And I don't care how god damn good you are at your job, you can't just treat the customers you don't like as if they were dog shit," bellowed Bob.

"Hey," said Aaron between bites. "I don't fire unless fired upon. I made a point with the lady and the tourist poser would have given you a shitty review regardless. I can spot douches like that a mile away. I would rather them say I suck for good reason than say your food is shit for no reason at all."

"That is not the point," said Bob, still fuming. "I have a business to run here and you have become a full-blown boil on my ass."

Finishing his pizza, Aaron tossed his plate before continuing. "Look, boss, I know I am a pain in the ass. Most of the costumers know I am a pain in the ass. But I take care of our regulars and I get people coming back. I promise I get you more business than I lose, and if that ever changes, I will see myself out," he said.

Bob slammed his fist on his desk. "Again, that is not the point! This is my fucking business and not yours! You do things my way, you hear? My way! You got that?"

"Crystally fucking clear," said Aaron.

"Good," said Bob as he tried to calm down. "Now, as a gesture of your goodwill and as an apology to me, you are going to go to the clinic downstairs and get the new vaccine," he said.

"I am sure as fuck not going to do that," said Aaron.

"Oh, you are," said Bob, pointing at him, "You are going to go, and you are going to do it with a god damn smile fucking smeared on your face. I want everyone getting it and if you go, the rest of them will follow. So, go take your break and then get the shot. And if you don't get the shot, then don't come back to work, cause you are fired and dead to me."

Aaron stood, taking off his apron. "Is there any option where I can keep my job and still be dead to you?" he asked.

"Get out!"

Aaron exited the office before walking toward the exit. David gave him a sage-like nod, knowing this was par for the course. Janette and the other employees either watched or shook their heads at him as he departed. Now free of the deli for a few moments, Aaron walked about, trying to decide what to do.

And as he walked, that is when he saw her.

She filled his view as soon as his pupils fixed on her, and that was soon all that he saw. Her fire-red hair flowing free as she walked back to her job. Aaron admired every facet of her from her soft skin to her curves that would not be denied, even obscured in work attire. And then, as he drew closer, she turned her head and her cool blue eyes fixed on his and they shared a moment.

"Just my fucking luck," she said as she quickened her pace.

Aaron gave chase. "Shawna, wait up!" he called out.

Hearing Aaron speak just made Shawna walk faster. This in turn slowed Aaron, for yes, he hated to see her go but loved watching her leave. At last, he sprinted up to walk beside her as she spoke to him without looking. "I thought I made it clear I don't want to talk to you," she said.

"Insanely clear," said Aaron. "But come on, already. It's been six damn months. I know I fucked up, but I am not going to ever make it right if you don't give me the chance."

"What makes you think I am ever going to give you another chance," she asked.

"Because you love me," he said smugger than he wanted to.

"Loved you, maybe. But that was then, and this is now. You screwed with my heart too many times," she said, just as harshly as she wanted to.

Keeping pace, Aaron took several steps to contain his emotions and wrestle down the right words. "Look, I know I was a dick. I took you for granted and I regret it completely. Can't you just give me one chance to show you I have changed?"

"No," she said firmly. "Because you haven't."

"But I have!"

She stopped and looked at him. "Are you still squatting at your brother's apartment?"

Aaron shrugged nervously. "Well yeah. For the moment anyway."

"Still playing video games till four in the morning and depending on others for rides and food?"

"Not all the time," he said proudly. "Some nights I hit the sack as early as three.

"You haven't changed a bit," said Shawna as she kept walking.

"But I have changed," said Aaron as he kept up with her. "I only do all that other shit because you are not around."

"It's been six months, you are just lonely and horny," she countered.

"Maybe I am those things, but that doesn't mean I am not lonely and horny for you," said Aaron. "What do I have to do to prove it isn't about just the sex, jimmy punch myself right now?"

"I could do it for you," she said in a quite sinister fashion.

Aaron held up his hands. "Hey, I am going to need to walk again sometime in the future. I don't think you would hold anything back."

Shawna shook her head. "You don't deserve restraint. And you haven't done anything but sulk and squat at your brother's place since I kicked you out. You haven't changed at all."

"Maybe you're right," he countered as he stepped in front of her. "I'm stuck. I have grown into a bigger dick than I ever could have imagined. But that's because I'm missing something from my life and it's got me pissed off at the world. I'm missing you. Can't you try and see that so we can attempt to fix this shit? Tell me what the hell I have to do!"

Shawna fixed him a hard stare as she removed strands of hair from her face. "You want to know what you have to do? You really want to know? I can assure you it will be impossible for you," she said.

"Just tell me," said Aaron.

Shawna crossed her arms as she practically looked at Aaron all the way to his soul. He tried to ignore how much the action accentuated her breasts, as this was a time for the game face. "Grow the fuck up, Aaron. Be a man. Take responsibility. It may be too late for us but that is how you stop fucking up the future," she said before she walked by him and away. This time he let her go, as much as it pained and pissed him off.

Kicking at a trash bin, Aaron then fumed as he walked about once more. He'd accepted that he had fucked up with Shawna. The problem was unfucking the situation was proving fruitless. He had to take a step forward and show her that he meant what he said. And while it seemed silly, he knew one thing he could do to further that cause.

Cursing himself and the world, Aaron made his way downstairs to get the Omega Vaccine.

4

JESUS? NAILED IT!

With a crisp morning in full glorious swing, Adam stopped his aimless wanderings at last. He had spent the entire evening thinking on the future of mankind. The fear he felt, the terror that was rising and causing humans to act out like angry, scared children haunted him. He'd tried many things in the past to guide them in the right direction. One path had been mostly successful, sending echoes of a message of understanding and love for hundreds of years. The fact that it had ended rather badly for Adam was immaterial.

At least that is what Adam was telling himself in that moment.

Adam had shirked his duties for far too long. The last time he had truly tried to make an impact on mankind, it was in one of the most benevolent forms he had ever assumed. Adam had streamlined his message, had made it simple enough for all to follow without doubt. And while his message had carried through the centuries, it had been punctuated by a pretty shitty crucifixion. Supreme being or not, you don't just get over shit like that easily.

Adam at last ceased his deep thoughts and wandering. Looking about, he discovered an alley that was unoccupied and entered it. With no one looking, Adam gathered his energies and harnessed them for the change. All the cells in his body modified and rearranged to fit his desired look. A brilliant light flooded the alley briefly before returning to normal. Adam gasped as he gathered himself once more. His strength returning, Adam stood and faced the sunlight. "It is done. And it has begun again," he said, with a new voice and renewed determination.

With his transformation complete, Adam exited the alley as Jesus of Nazareth.

As the morning hit him, Adam's brown skin glistened in the sunlight. It was a feature he added for effect and it always helped grab attention. His dark hair played upon his shoulders as he rubbed at the return of a beard. He was even donning the robes of old and allowing his scars to really show their depth as he prepared for his new mission. He would reach out to his people one at a time and, like ripples on the pond, he would spread his message of love once more.

Of course, social media wouldn't hurt the cause if he could make this shit go viral.

Taking the world in with new perspective and purpose, Adam (aka Jesus), strolled now in humble clothes and worn sandals. Never had he made a character with so much backstory before. Through his Jesus identity, Adam had been born, lived, and ultimately died. It was the most diehard bout of method acting there ever was, rivaling even Christian Bale and Daniel Day Lewis, thank you very much. And just like a deep, immersing character, you never were the same again afterwards.

Walking the streets, Adam started getting attention in the form of curious eyes. As he passed a group of coworkers walking together, he held up a hand. "Rejoice, my children, and be glad, for I have returned to you at last," he said.

"And who are you again?" one of them asked as he gave Adam a generous bubble for personal space.

Adam could not hide his surprise at not being immediately recognized. "It is I, Jesus, my child. The one who gave his life for your sins, spilt his blood for your salvation. And I have returned to you now in the darkest of times to bring you hope and light," said Adam quite lovingly.

One of the women of the bunch held out her hands as she quickened her pace. "Um, you are really freaking us out, sir. Please leave us alone or we will have to call the cops," she said as the scurried off.

As they distanced themselves from Adam, he could hear the first one mutter "That son of a bitch needs Jesus bad."

"But I *am* Jesus!" cried Adam to them to no avail. Trying not to take it personal, Adam pressed on.

With more walking, Adam came across an aging couple. The woman was pushing the man who was confined to a wheelchair. This saddened Adam, so he walked over and placed his hand on the man's head. The man was frozen by the touch for a moment as Adam filled him with his energy. "Arise and walk, my child," said Adam sagely.

The man looked at Adam in disbelief before he shook his head clear. Looking down at his legs, the man braced himself on his wheelchair and put his feet on the ground. With a look of pure amazement, he stood on his own. His face revealed pure awe and complete gratitude. His eyes teared up as he wished to express his thanks.

That was when his wife chimed in. "You motherfucker! I knew you were holding out on me all this time!" she roared before pushing her husband and storming off. "We're through!"

The man looked at Adam again. "Thanks a lot, man!" he then turned and chased after his wife. "But baby! I don't know what happened. That guy healed me or some shit! I swear!"

Adam continued to administer good deeds and the good word to little avail. Before long, most people on the street gave him a wide berth, often crossing to the other side to avoid him. He tried friendliness, compassion, and love but succeeded at none of them. He was starting to feel like a bumbling idiot.

A little flustered, Adam sat himself next to a homeless man, who was begging for change. The man was adorned in ragged clothes, a scraggly beard that went down his chest, and faded eyes that had obviously gained much wisdom through pain. The man was painfully honest, holding up a sign that read *Already Eaten. Beer Money Would be Nice. God Bless*. The two exchanged a long glance as those passing by returned to ignoring them completely.

“New at this, aren’t you?” asked the homeless man.

“Yes and no,” said Adam as he looked about. “It’s been some time. Never have I felt so much negativity and this is coming from someone who has been crucified.”

The homeless man’s eyes lit up. “Oh, you are into the kinky stuff. I saw a man at a leather camp that got off on that sort of thing. I passed of course, but it gets one curious,” he said wisely as he offered his hand, dirtied and holding fingerless gloves. “I’m Burt by the way,” said Burt, obviously.

Adam looked at the hand for a moment before he slowly shook it. “Jesus,” he said distantly. “Of Nazareth.”

Burt leaned back against the wall, chuckling to himself. “Well, welcome back, J.C.” he said between laughs. “It’s been an ever-growing shit show since you've been gone." Burt then offered him a bottle of filtered water. "Here, you can use this."

"Thank you, Burt," said Adam. "By why aren't you afraid? Why don't you scoff me like the others?"

Burt shrugged. "I guess it's perspective, J.C. I see things differently from down here. And you mean well. I haven't figured out if you are crazy or not yet, but you have been trying to do good for a while now. And the world needs more of that."

Adam swirled the contents of the water in the bottle before he continued. "So you are not convinced that I am in fact who I say I am?"

Burt shrugged. "Not my business either way, but I am not going to accuse you one way or the other," he said.

"Let me show you," said Adam, as he reached his hand over and placed it across Burt's eyes.

The transfer of energy was almost instantaneous, and Adam removed his hand as if it were nothing. But in that moment, Burt saw with the eyes he had in his twenties. The vibrant colors he remembered flooded back to him as well as the distance. He looked about like a child in wide-eyed wonderment. "Well fuck me running, J.C., cause you've sold me," said Burt as he continued to look about. "Thank you. it's nice to know that Jesus can take the time out and love a dub like me."

Adam sighed. "I love everyone, Burt. That is kind of my thing," he said as he ran his hand over the water bottle. Instantly the clear contents turned a deep crimson. Adam them offered the bottle back to Burt. "Would you like some wine?"

"Don't mind if I do," said Burt as he took the bottle and took a swing, taking a moment to marvel at the contents. "Holy hot Christ, Jesus, that's some good shit right there."

"Of course," said Adam. "I'm Jesus after all. You can't convince anyone by making shoddy wine," he offered.

"I'll drink to that," said Burt as he threw back the contents of the bottle in his hand. "Hot damn, J.C., you know how to make a man's day. I wish I could repay the favor in some way."

"You have already shown kindness and understanding where others have not. I am discovering it has become an even rarer commodity in this time," said Adam.

"That's the damn truth, J.C.," said Burt as he held up the last bit of the wine in a toast. "Times are tough. This world's going to hell in a handbag. I've a feeling everyone is going to be as screwed as I am soon enough. But at least we are all going to be in the same boat."

"How do you mean, my child?" asked Adam.

Burt scratched his beard before pointing to Adam. "Well there is all this talk about the Mayan Calendar end of times. People are all sorts of crazy about it right now. Riots. Parties. People giving less and less fucks as the day looms closer. And now you are here. I figure the Rapture is upon us, like the bible said," he replied.

"You know, it always seemed egotistical to look at my message in the bible," said Adam thoughtfully. "I was just always relieved that it carried on through the years."

Burt rummaged in his bag and procured a battered bible before running his hands over it. "I always tried to follow the message, which to me was boiled down to love one another," said Burt.

Adam smiled at him in a very Jesus-like fashion. "That was the message, Burt. For if you love others as I have loved you, there would be no room for wickedness, and there would be peace," he said.

Burt offered a dirty, tooth-filled grin as he shrugged. "I won't lie though, sometimes I slip, but I do my best to follow the ten commandments," he stated.

"Wait, the what?" asked Adam.

Burt looked at him curiously. "The ten commandments handed down to Moses from God himself. Hey, it's all in the bible, J.C.," said the homeless man before handing the bible to Adam.

Adam began looking over the contents of Burt's bible, becoming more and more dismayed by the second. "No. No, this isn't right. This here is misquoted. I never said that. That was taken out of context. And there is much missing. What has happened?" said Adam, now completely beside himself.

Burt shrugged helplessly. "The world is a fan and the shit has finally hit it, I suppose," he said sagely.

Adam kept flipping pages. "But this is…this makes no sense," he said, still reading. "This all could be left to interpretation, used to further someone's agenda. This isn't a guide, this is confinement and division!" He paused on one part, widening his eyes. "And if Eve ever found out she was blamed for sin there would be a wrath set upon this world like you have never seen."

"Bible not to your liking then?" asked Burt.

Adam shook his head. "Not at all. Mine was a message of love and didn't require a whole book to express. How could anyone love thy neighbor with all the judgments and divisions set upon them with this? Love was the whole point of everything, Burt. My disciples were sinners. Everyone 'sins,' so to speak. Love was the triumph, not war and separation. This hurts me more than the crucifixion," stammered Adam.

"Or marriage," stated Burt with a shiver.

Adam grew fixated on a particular section of the bible before he shook his head in fury. “And what is up with Leviticus?! The insanity I have read so far is astounding!”

Burt nodded in understanding. “Right fucking up there with Deuteronomy. Careful Jesus, you’ll get an ulcer or hives. And that is possibly a blemish that would make you unworthy to worship god according to Leviticus,” he said.

“I can take no more, it’s too much” said Adam, slamming the book shut.

“Forgive me, J.C., but that is definitely what she said too,” said Burt with a wink.

“What?”

“Never mind. I’m going to hell anyway,” said Burt.

Adam stood then, clearly shaken. “I must do something about this, end the insanity, and lead my flock in the right direction again,” he said.

Burt watched him for a second. “Just be careful. Sometimes people don’t want to go in the right direction, especially if it is hard or not profitable. I think your first attempt showed that pretty well.”

“Indeed,” said Adam, as he looked about. “But I must try. It is a time of great and perilous darkness and we stand at the precipice of doom. And…” Suddenly Adam trailed off as revelation filled his eyes. “Ah, yes, what she said. I get it now.”

Burt pointed at Adam and grinned. “Loving, understanding, and sharp as nails,” he said before hiccupping and covering his mouth. He then pointed to Adam’s hands. “Sorry, that was out of line.”

Adam looked about the street as he spoke. “I am not without a sense of humor, Burt, I assure you. That is why there are things like the platypus and premature ejaculation.”

"A fair point," said Burt as he handed Adam another bottle. Without paying much mind, Adam turned it into wine before handing it back to Burt. "So, what will do you now?"

"I must find a place where my message will be heard swiftest," said Adam.

Burt took a drink as he thought on that. "You know, we aren't far off from a megachurch. I understand they have been running Saturday services with all the hoopla going on. I bet that would be a great place to start."

Adam looked at him curiously. "A megachurch?"

Burt nodded. "Yeah. Called Christ and the Resurrection. Bout two miles south of here. Big sumbitch. Can't miss it, J.C.," he offered.

Adam looked in the direction Burt was pointing. "Thank you, Burt. This should be…interesting to say the least," he said.

"Their pictures of you don't do you justice," said Burt.

"The rarely do in these parts," said Adam as he offered his hand to Burt. "I want to thank you again, Burt. But this is where we must part ways."

Burt stood and shook Adam's hand. "Pleasure's been all mine, J.C., and I wish you the best of luck."

"One more thing before I go," said Adam as he focused himself upon Burt. Suddenly all the pains and aches of Burt's body dissolved, and the man felt twenty years younger. "It is the least I can do," added Adam.

Burt beamed at him. "Hot damn, J.C., you've made my year," he said as he moved about. "I've not felt this damn good in ages."

"And you will continue to feel that way for some time, for your body and spirit have been rejuvenated," said Adam.

Burt could not help himself and gave Adam a hug. "Damn, man. You're the best," he said before releasing Adam. "You need some help on this foray? Need a disciple or something or other?"

Adam shook his head. "No, my child," he replied before turning and narrowing his eyes. "This is something I must do alone. Farewell to you, Burt.

"Bye, Jesus," said Burt, waving. "Hope to see you again sometime."

Burt watched as Adam walked with determination toward the megachurch. He still couldn't believe his luck or how youthful he felt in those moments. He truly believed that he had just met Jesus Christ and would never forget this moment for all of eternity. Of course, he sobered up a bit when he thought about where J.C. was heading.

"Shitballs, they are gonna hate his ass," said Burt sadly.

With his strength and will, it didn't take long for Adam to reach the Christ and the Resurrection Church. He barreled right passed the gawkers and onlookers, shelving his message for now. He was inherently curious about the prospect of a megachurch and was none too keen about what it possibly entailed. Rounding a corner, Adam laid his eyes on it.

At the spectacle before him he murmured, "Art thou shitting me?"

Adam stood, robbed of composure as he stared at the church. The building sprawled out from a focal entrance adorned with the biggest god damn cross Adam had ever seen. The church could easily fit thousands of people, and it was practically swelling today. The pageantry of it all was unsettling. Adam observed the casual devoted as they sauntered about, as if such a spectacle was completely normal.

Adam then made his way slowly toward the church. He tunneled his vision, focusing solely on the doors before him now, trying to stay distracted from the utter opulence that stood before him. As he approached, he garnered several sets of eyes upon him. Surprisingly, few paid him much mind, as if seeing him was nothing out of the ordinary.

"Oh, we must be having a play today," said one of the onlookers.

"Must be one of the wise men or something," said another before calling out to Adam. "Excuse me, sir, can we get a picture with you?"

Adam held up a hand. "Not now, my child. There is work that must be done," he said before reaching the doors of the church.

Adam could hear the man handling the rejection behind him poorly. "I just wanted a selfie with you! God!" he exclaimed.

"If he only knew," mumbled Adam.

Upon entering the megachurch, Adam was greeted by people at the door who did doubletakes at his attire. The greeters then exchanged glances, shrugging their shoulders as they watched Adam look upon the church's insides. What he saw almost brought tears to Adam's eyes, cause being back in the form of Jesus always had a way of hitting him extra hard in the feels department.

Adam let his eyes dance about, absorbing every new surprise and atrocity as it assaulted his senses. He was standing in a very fancy lobby, in front of a welcome desk where three people sitting watched him suspiciously. Beyond that were tables with people sitting and eating snacks. To the right was a café filled with overpriced selections and generic coffee smells. To the left was what appeared to be a gift shop. Beyond that, Adam could hear a pastor giving a sermon that was punctuated with several amens and halleluiahs.

From behind the welcome desk, a balding, middle-aged man stood and offered a painstakingly fake smile to Adam. "Hello, sir. Welcome to the Church of Christ and the Resurrection. How can we help you?" he asked.

Adam shook his head, still looking about. "It is actually I who have come to help you, though I don't know yet if I can," he replied.

"I see," said the man, evaluating Adam sternly. "Are you part of a skit or play? Reverend Thomas did not inform us of any such activities today."

Adam shook his head. "This is no skit or play," he said in all seriousness. "I have come to save you if I can, as I promised long ago."

"Okay then," said the man as he pointed to the desk. "Since you are new why don't you fill out a nametag so people know who you are, and we will get you a program."

Adam shook his head as he picked up a sharpie and scrawled on one of the nametag stickers. Sighing, he removed the sticker and placed it upon his robes. The tag simply read: *Jesus, yes THAT one*. The people behind the counter gasped as they read it, obviously thinking it sacrilegious that Adam would dare put such a thing.

The balding man's chest huffed out as he looked sternly at Adam. "Sir, we do not take kindly to people jesting or making fun of our lord and savior. I am afraid I am going to have to ask you to leave," he said.

Adam looked at him with pain. "My son, you wouldn't know the second coming if it fell from the sky and crucified you itself," he said. "I please ask you to rest yourself and let me do my work. The world and my flock need me now more than ever."

"I will give you once more chance, sir. And then I will have to call security," said the balding man.

Adam's balked. "You have security? You filter who can and cannot enter this place of worship?"

"We have to ensure the safety and message of our flock," said the man, crossing his arms. "I suggest you leave now and think about your decisions."

"I've had countless years to weigh my decisions, child," said Adam as he walked around the welcome desk. "I must now see what passes as fellowship here."

The man came out of the enclosed area and grabbed Adam's arm. "I am afraid I can't let you do that, sir," he said.

Adam looked at his nametag. "William, is it? Well, William, I must say something I often do not to those of my flock," he said as he placed a hand on William's head. "Sit and say nothing, my son," he said.

At the request and surge of energy rushing through him, William's body convulsed before he fell on his ass and went limp. As the other two behind the counter came to assist William, they saw the man staring up at the ceiling with childlike wonder, not a care in the world resting on his face. He easily resembled an infant staring gleefully at the mobile spinning above his crib. The woman behind the counter took William's head and placed it on her lap before looking at Adam angrily. "What have you done to him?" she yelled.

Adam offered the woman a gentle smile of assurance. "Given him peace. I assure you that he is fine," he said. "Now please leave me so that I may see what must be seen."

Thus free of further distraction, Adam made his way to the service already in progress. The sight of it struck him as hard as any nail on his flesh. There before him where enough pews for a few thousand worshippers. The stage was lit up like a concert, adorned with large screens, instruments, and mics. There was no altar, but a man in a sharp suit addressed those in attendance with passion as he spoke into the mic that rested on his ear and mouth. His face was magnified on the screens upon him so that all could see his glory.

Adam knew this had to be Pastor Thomas.

Pastor Thomas paced slowly about on the stage, with all eyes and spotlights upon him. His dark blue custom suit and hair were both cut perfectly. He was an attractive man in his early thirties and his actions and words demanded the attention of those in attendance. Yet there was something about him almost immediately that did not sit well with Adam, and so the ancient being listened patiently for the moment.

"Brothers and sisters," exclaimed Pastor Thomas as he continued his sermon. "As the news has shown you, as the papers have shown you, as the words of others have shown you, we have reached dark times. The world trembles in fear as we stand before the gates of judgment, where we must stand devotedly, for we are the faithful, are we not?"

The pastor's words were met with many screams of amen. Adam watched on.

"Now, we may not be able to know the Lord's will, but that does not excuse us from doing the Lord's work. And that is why we are here, is it not? It is through your faith and through your support that we may reach out to those unprepared for our Lord and Savior. And through your generosity we may have a chance at bringing them to the light and salvation!"

"Praise Jesus!" said a bulk of the congregation in unison.

Pastor Thomas continued. "With every bit of support you give, we grow stronger in the Lord. With every person who receives the message, we can take solace in the fact that we have saved one more soul from the fires of damnation and elevated the glory of his name. Now brothers and sisters, I cannot tell you if this is the end or not. That is not for me to say. What I can say is that this is a new beginning for our flock and a time we will be as one with our message!"

More praises and cheers met the pastor's words. Adam felt his scarred fists clenching but remained stiff as a board.

"And I know what you are asking yourselves," said Pastor Thomas, pressing ever onward. "You are asking yourselves how can you show your support? How can you make a difference? Well let me tell you, my brothers and sisters, for every dollar you donate, for every new person you bring to the flock and for every one of my books that you purchase here or on line, you give power to our message! You add to our reach and the possibilities we possess become stronger and vaster! It is through your generosity that we show the world we are devoted, that our souls are saved, and we stand as one for the Lord and wait for his triumphant return! Can I get an amen?"

"Amen!" thundered the congregation.

"You most certainly cannot!" thundered Adam.

The depth and power of Adam's voice stunned the large crowd and thousands of eyes turned upon him. Adam walked down the aisle and toward the gleaming pastor upon the stage. Pastor Thomas held up his hands for quiet and calm, but there was something about Adam's presence that unsettled him. Adam did not take the stage, yet he stood before it as he addressed Pastor Thomas.

With the crowd's attention upon him, Adam spoke again, and did not need a microphone to be heard. "You stand upon this false altar spewing words and claims, yet all I see is greed in your eyes and for your flock. This is not the message, nor is it the way."

Pastor Thomas smiled nervously as he tried to soothe the congregation. "Ladies and gentlemen, it appears that we have a guest to our service today," he said before pointing to

Adam. “And who might you be, sir? Please state your name for the congregation.”

“I am Jesus of Nazareth,” said Adam adamantly. “And I have returned to you now in this dark hour to bring you again toward the light.”

Adam’s response brought a series of gasps and chuckles from the crowd as they tried to figure out if this was really happening or if it was some skit put on by the pastor. Pastor Thomas smiled as he spoke again. “Do you hear that? This man claims to be your risen savior.”

“I claim nothing but the truth,” said Adam as he looked at the crowd. “In my time, I never needed a church for my flock. I wandered. I came to you. I fed and cared for you as I offered you my message. I certainly didn’t take your money, nor did I require compensation for my message! This man, this pastor, only elevates himself with your offerings.”

As his flock began to talk amongst themselves, Pastor Thomas fought the color rising to his cheeks. He stared angrily at Adam before pointing accusingly. "You sir, are a liar and a fake. There is no way that you are the risen Christ!"

Adam raised a curious eyebrow as he placed his hands at his hips. "And what makes you so sure, my child?"

Pastor Thomas refocused upon his flock as he pointed at Adam. "Can you not see the falsehood, this wolf in sheep's clothing? He is an imposter I say, sent to us from the devil himself if he is not Satan in the flesh! Do not let his forked tongue sway your ears! See through his deceptions!"

"I believe I am still waiting for reasons to go along with this banter," said Adam patiently.

Pastor turned angrily upon Adam then. "Look at your skin, imposter. You are not even white! We Americans know the truth of the matter."

This brought a mixed reaction from the crowd. Pastor Thomas may have been a white guy, but he was starting to show his true colors. Adam watched him for a second, cocking his head. While as Jesus he held infinite patience, the man on the stage before him was doing a good job of boning that.

Adam tried once more. "Yes, of course you do," said Adam shaking his head. I cannot even begin to tell you about all the Caucasians that we beheld within Nazareth back in the day," he offered before turning to the congregation. "Do you not see, my children? This is why I have returned in my original form, so that I could know that you understand the message, that love sees no color, that love sees all in the same, unjudging light. That is the purpose and the message. Forget the commandments! You only need one and is to love one another as I have loved you. That covers everything you need to know. If I were to add one update to this, it would be stop being dickish to each other. It is getting ridiculous!"

Adam waited as his words sent the congregation to silence. The only sound was heavy breathing coming from the speakers compliments of Pastor Thomas. Adam looked about, hopeful that his words were sinking in, hopeful that this was the starting point of a new era. At last, words called back to him from the back pews.

"Jesus was white!"

"White Jesus!"

"He was an American too!" spouted another. Most of the crowd focused on the direction of that voice, though no one was bold enough to claim that little kernel of lunacy.

At last, Adam could take no more as he leaped upon the stage. Pastor Thomas rushed away, obviously frightened by Adam. Adam then looked disapprovingly upon the crowd, hurt and angered by their lack of compassion and reasoning skills. Adam had not felt this mad in hundreds of years, if ever.

"This is not a house of god!" Adam exclaimed. "This is not a place of love! This has become a selfish den of thieves, and you should know how I feel about dens for thieves," he said before turning his head at Pastor Thomas. "And you are their master," he accused.

Pastor Thomas tried to suppress his growing resentment. "Heathen! You spout lies in the house of the Lord! For this you will be dealt with," he challenged strongly. "Security!"

Adam stood in front of the pastor then, shaking his head. "Your greed has made you hungry. And you have fed that hunger too well. To think all of the good you could have done with this money. The ministry, the feeding of the poor, the helping the downtrodden. Yet you think status and numbers are the symbol of prominence and glory. And you are wrong," he said.

Pastor Thomas grabbed Adam by his robes, attempting to pull him off the stage. "Enough of you! I'll throw you off this stage if I have to!"

Adam shook his head. "You will do no such things, especially not with that strength," he said. "Now unhand me."

"Fuck off!" screamed Pastor Thomas. The words echoed through the auditorium, causing the pastor's cheeks to flare up with embarrassment. "Get off my stage! These are my flock!"

"I said unhand me, pastor," said Adam.

"Get out of here!"

Adam sighed again. "So be it," he said as he squatted slightly.

Now positioned properly, Adam drove an open palm into the stomach of Pastor Thomas. The man immediately released Adam, clutching at his guts. He moaned like a trapped whale, fed with Viagra and kept mere feet from poonanny. Soon his pants were doused in deep crimson as the liquid covered most of his trousers and poured down his legs. Pastor Thomas collapsed on the floor, wailing in agony as his congregation offered a collective gasp.

Yet as horrified as they were, none of them were missing this show. They had paid up on the apocalypse after all.

"Holy shit, god dammit all to fucking hell, that burns! It burns!" cried Pastor Thomas.

"He's bleeding to death," cried one of the approaching guards.

Adam shook his head. "Not at all. You now see, Pastor Thomas, as your full bladder has proven to you, that it is not just water I can turn into wine," he said.

Pastor Thomas could not contain himself any longer. “You rat bastard! You damn son of a bitch! Guards! Tear him apart!”

As a score of security finally hit the stage, Adam shook his head. “Not this day,” he said adamantly as his eyes narrowed. “Today I cleanse this church.”

Drawing his hands to himself, Adam unfurled them. When he did, both of his fists were clutching the tails of large fish. As the security guards rushed him, Adam began pelting them deftly with the conjured aquatic life. Proving himself quite adept with them, Adam had struck two security guards in the face before the others could blink an eye. Adam them flailed the fish in a way that would give Michelangelo a run for his money as he dealt with the security and random members of the congregation hungry to get in on the action.

Within moments, the stage was an all-out melee. Feeling hearty and driven by the action, more and more disciples rushed up to the stage to face Adam. Adam endured them all in Zen, Jesus-like fashion. That is, if Jesus was the star of Fist of Fury instead of Bruce Lee. The wise members who remained in the pews were in for a show as Adam fought the circling enemies, wailing on them with large, conjured fish, conjuring more when they became too mushy. Some even rushed to grab snacks.

Pastor Thomas crawled painfully off the stage as another security guard went flying over him. Adam stood at the ready among the remaining people that still wanted a piece of him. Several felled individuals were strewn across the stage and the aisles. Body parts and innards of fish were smeared about throughout the mix and the fish smell was starting to permeate. Adam conjured two more fresh fish in his hands as he prepared for the next round with those still holding to their bravery.

"Are there any other non-believers?" asked Adam expectantly. The deity had been a message of love, guidance, and understanding over hundreds upon hundreds of years. He had to admit that it was nice blowing off some steam for a change.

"Get him!" yelled one of the security guards still standing.

The emboldened men charged once more. Adam let the readied fish in his hands do their magic, lashing out, striking faces most harshly. Men fell to the ground with fish scales and often guts on their faces. Adam slapped the biggest of the guards with a fish, spinning him around before kicking him in his ass and off the stage. It was clear by now to the congregation that Adam was not fucking around. Many on the stage started to flee and those watching in the pews joined them.

"Where are you going?" Adam asked to the fleeing masses as he wrapped a fish around the neck of a staggering man before hurling him away. "Where is your condemnation now? Where is the self-righteousness that fueled you?"

As only screams met his question, Adam conjured more fish, though smaller this time. He hurled these fish at those fleeing, pelting them in their backs or heads with surprisingly deadly accuracy. And while the fish were by no means lethal force, they still stung like the dickens and left their fishy declaration upon any who were struck. "You have been judged," declared Adam, still pelting people with conjured fish as he walked. "Live and realize your sins so that you may walk away from wickedness."

"He's fucking crazy! Run!" screamed a man, pointing at Adam.

Adam nailed the man between the eyes with a conjured trout. "Judged!"

"The devil is upon us," bellowed a woman as she pushed down two of her congregation to get away faster.

"Judged!" thundered Adam as he hit her in the back of the head with a bass.

Brandishing a flag pole, a viral man found bravery from arming himself. "You are going down, asshole!" he exclaimed as he swung the pole at Adam's head.

Casually, Adam caught the pole with his left hand before conjuring a fish in his right. He shook his head at the young man, pitying his youthful foolishness. "Judged," said Adam as he walloped the man with a walleye. As the young man crumbled on the floor, Adam conjured two catfish, throwing them on the man. "Judged again and then further judged."

By this time, the masses were fleeing in droves. Adam walked behind them, hurling more fish as he went. Soon they were in the hallway again where Adam shifted his focus. He first set his eyes on the gift shop. Full of a book written by Pastor Thomas and other spiritual odds and ends, Adam could not stand the sight of it. Holding his arms above his head, he conjured a very large tuna before tossing it through the glass display before him. Adam then conjured himself two more long catfish in his hands before shifting his focus on the cafe.

Proceeding to a disturbance call at the Christ the Resurrection Church, Officer Frank Wagner pulled into the parking lot amidst a shit storm. Bringing his patrol car to a stop, Officer Wagner watched as hundreds of men and woman flooded out of the large church of worship, screaming for their lives. Wagner sighed. It had been a busy fucking month to say the least. The world was going to hell in a handbasket and there just wasn't enough cops to be everywhere.

Amidst the fleeing flock of what he would refer to as "bible thumpers," Officer Wagner exited his vehicle and accessed the situation. Yeah, it was a clusterfuck all right. People screaming for Jesus to save them while others raved it was Jesus they needed saved from. Wagner was worried at first when he saw people hobbling away covered in blood. But upon further investigation he would discover blood and scales belonging to what the perp was apparently using to assault the congregation.

Wading through the stream of insanity, Officer Wagner found a face he recognized in Pastor Thomas. The pastor was hunched over in pain as he limped away from his church. The entire front of his pants was covered in red, like the man had pissed wine all over himself. Granted, Wagner knew that was impossible, but he called them like he saw them. He rushed over to Pastor Thomas to assist him. Apparently, every step was agony for the man of god as he moved still as fast as his pain would allow him.

As Officer Wagner supported him, Pastor Thomas breathed a sigh of pure relief between gasps. "Thank the Lord you are here, officer. God be praised!"

"What the hell is going on in there?" asked Officer Wagner as back up pulled into the parking lot as well.

Pastor Thomas gasped. "It's the devil himself! Look what he has done to my church! Look what he has done to me! It burns, the bastard! It still burns!"

"Is he armed?" asked Wagner.

"Yes," spat the pastor.

"Knife? Guns? Blunt weapons?"

"No. Fish."

"....Fish?"

"Yes, fish, god damnit! Oh, and he looks like Jesus, but darker."

"Well this can't get any weirder," said Officer Wagner. He then turned in time to see a Goliath Grouper fish fall from the sky and smash the piss out of his patrol car. "Well obviously I was fucking wrong."

Just then, the sky began to rain a storm of fish. Bluegill, trout, bass, perch, and crappie fell from the clouds, slapping fleeing members of the flock and splashing upon the ground. Fish guts and screams filled the parking lot as Officer Wagner stood and shielded his head. He reached for his gun, yet as he saw the perpetrator emerge from the church, he hesitated, for the scene had gotten super surreal as fuck.

I mean, Wagner thought he had seen just about every damn thing the world had to offer as a policeman, but now he knew he was dead ass wrong.

There, exiting the church and walking angrily toward Officer Wagner was what appeared to be Jesus Christ himself. His dark skin was covered in sweat. His tattered robes and sandals were spotted with fish blood. Perspiration fell from his brow and his beard as he scowled at the fleeing churchgoers. In his right hand was a half-beaten salmon. In his right, he cradled a coffee dispenser.

Officer Wagner rubbed at his eyes and slapped his own face, feeling like the raining fish had been enough to put him over the edge. But no, here was an angry Jesus armed with a sashimi grade fish and enough coffee to caffeinate a classroom, looking like he was ready to smite a motherfucker at the drop of a hat. It was weird. It was strange. And it was the icing on the shit cake of his week.

Approaching this Jesus man, Officer Wagner held out a hand, indicating to the man that he had come far enough. "Alright, buddy, I gotta know. What's your story?" he asked.

Suddenly, the anger that had clouded the man faded as he looked at the policeman mournfully. "I am sorry. For the first time in centuries I truly felt my anger. And it bested me. I don't know what to say. I feel remorse and shame, mainly because I rather enjoyed it," said the Jesus.

"Hey, we all have hard days, pal," said Wagner as he motioned to the forcefully tenderized salmon. Why don't you put down the fish and we can talk this out, okay?"

The Jesus man looked down in his hand, slowly releasing the fish. The salmon somehow looked grateful for the release, able to die with some shred of dignity. "Yes, yes of course. This was not my intent, my son. I had come to spread the good word, that I had returned to guide my children back upon the righteous path. Yet I have started in the wrong direction completely."

Officer Wagner kept his hands out casually and remained cool as a cucumber. "Well, let's talk about it then, and not have any more violence today," he said.

The Jesus man nodded softly. "I would like that. I abhor violence. I am a man of love, actually. I simply cannot tolerate greed and intolerance. That has been my stance since the start."

"Well, what do you say I grab some cups and we drink some of that coffee and figure this out?" asked Officer Wagner.

The man Jesus nodded to him with a glimmer of a smile. "Yes. Yes, I would like that very much, my son. Bless you and your kindness in a dark and strange time for me," he said.

"Shoot his ass, officer!" bellowed Pastor Thomas.

The man Jesus pointed angrily at him. "Silence yourself, sinner! Heathen, who flourishes in a den if thievery and sin, hold your tongue this instant!"

And like that a gunshot went off. Officer Wagner jumped and reached again for his gun. The man Jesus flinched as a powerful pinging sound echoed thunderously. Wagner looked back at his back up. There leaning on his car's hood with a smoking barrel was Officer Lane Creasy. The man was a youthful, trigger-happy, nervous wreck. And as he just proved, he was an accident waiting to happen.

Officer Wagner turned back to look on the man Jesus, who was in turn looking at the coffee dispenser and the trove of black gold that was leaking from the bullet hole. The Jesus looked between Officer Creasy and the slain coffee dispenser. The storm clouds began a brewing again as the smell of fish returned. Wagner watched amazed as two large catfish materialized in the supposed messiah's hands.

"You, treacherous fuckers of mothers," said the Jesus as he began to twirl the fish in his hands. "This war for salvation is just getting started."

"Oh shit," said Officer Wagner.

And then, once more, Jesus charged into the fray, catfish swinging as gunshots erupted and fish began to rain on the parking lot again.

5

INSANITY SETS SAIL

Sitting in his boss's office, Brandon sat quietly as Jim bandaged his hand. With the prospect of blood gone, he was just about back to normal. And as such, he could barely look at his boss in the eyes. Instead, he sipped his water as Jim finished his work.

"So," started Jim as he eyed his handiwork. "How do you think you handled that, Brandon?" he asked.

Brandon drew a long breath and replied as he exhaled. "If I had to sum it up in one word, Jim, I would have to say crappily," he breathed.

"And how could you have handled it better?"

"Pretty much any other way than I did. I need to offer a post-coital cigarette to the pooch I screwed out there," said Brandon.

Jim thought on Brandon's words as he went and sat behind his desk. The office was every bit as dorky as the shop Jim ran. It held multiple fields of nerd culture, from action figures to posters and items that were either far too valuable to have out on display or he was too reluctant to part with. For long moments Jim watched Brandon as his employee held firm in his apologetic stance.

"Brandon," he started as he repositioned his vintage Batman figurine, "I know it can be tough to work here sometimes. The clientele just isn't the same as it used to be. But we are at the mercy of the times. We still have a great base and I would hate to have to up and move after spending so much time and effort getting established here."

Brandon nodded as he pointed back to the front. "Boss, I fully understand. I take full responsibility for my fuck-ups. I really don't know what came over me. I love this job. I love working with you and the gang. I guess I just hate what this mall has become, and it got to me more than it should have. I tried to hold out, but that last pompous dad just put me right over the damn edge. I will fall on my sword now if you wish. But blindfold me so the sight of my own blood doesn't kill my last shred of dignity," he said.

"I don't think that will be necessary," said Jim chuckling. "And don't think I don't understand. We are well beyond this mall's golden age for sure. There will likely come a day when shops like these will be no more. If Mr. Whitworth had his way, all the last hold-outs would be gone tomorrow."

"Short-sighted, selfish pig," mumbled Brandon. "He's taking his mall down the yuppie highway to hell. But that still doesn't excuse my actions. I will take whatever punishment you deem fit, Jim."

Jim sighed. "It's not easy to stay mad at you, Brandon, especially when you are quick to take fault for your actions. I am going to chock this up as a momentary lapse of sanity, not to happen again. But I want you to go home and get some rest and come back to me tomorrow rested and refreshed. Is that clear?"

Brandon stood, nodding. "Crystal clear, Jim," he said, offering his hand. "And it won't happen again. You have my word."

Jim stood and shook Brandon's hand. "Good. Now go get some rest, son. You might need it more than you realize. And be careful out there. The world's not showing any signs of improving yet."

"You're telling me," said Brandon as he exited the office. "See you tomorrow, boss."

Leaving the store, Brandon gave a salute to his coworker Jay. Jay offered him a grin and thumbs up, clearly pleased with how Brandon had reacted. Brandon shook his head and headed to the parking lot. Walking by the perturbed man and his family as he did so. The father scowled at him, yet smugly, looking like he was proud of his formal complaint.

"Just so you know, sir, I still very much have my job," said Brandon with a grin. "And now that I am off the clock, I will bid you a kind go-fuck-yourself and be on my way," he said before looking at the man's son. "As for you, take a good look at your dad and make the conscious effort to not be him, for the entire world's sake," he finished before he was off. The man wanted to go after Brandon, but his wife held to his arm, begging not to make a scene.

Making his way to his car, Brandon started home. He was kind of excited at the prospect, as there was a strong possibility that he would have the place to himself for a while. Some alone time was exactly what he needed. With everyone else at work, his sudden breakdown may have turned into exactly what he needed.

Now driving, Brandon turned his music back on, desiring it to fill his senses. But even with some bitchin' music blaring in the background, he could not help but notice the weird shit and trouble a brewing outside his window. Brandon couldn't quite place it at first, but something wasn't right. It was just a grim feeling at first, but the more he drove, the more things increased in their weirdness.

"What the actual fuck?" said Brandon as he slowed to process the scene coming from a gas station parking lot.

There, at the Mighty Quick gas station, Brandon saw three police cars surrounding a man at the pumps. The man was walking stiffly, apparently yelling incoherently. In his right hand was a squeegee and in his left the nozzle to a gas pump. Gas flowed from it like a fount as the man paced back and forth in agitated confusion. The bravest of the officers was inching toward the man, ordering him to lay on the ground. In his hand he had his taser gun at the ready.

"Oh, I wouldn't do that if I were you," said Brandon as he quickly sped away. He had no intention of being close to that situation when it went to shit.

The explosion that followed some seconds later indicated that it did.

The remainder of the drive was no picnic either. Brandon saw many things in that time, and few were moments that he would dub normal. There was a man drooling profusely as he hung on to some lady's hood, dry humping her vehicle like there was no tomorrow. The lady, obviously unnerved, kept driving. There was another man walking similarly to the man at the Mighty Quick, lumbering after a group of women clumsily. The bulge in his pants indicated his limbs weren't the only thing that were stiff.

Another mile down, a woman was standing in front of a restaurant engaged in a fight with four men. Brandon thought about stopping when he realized that the woman was not only winning, but easily so. She threw one of the men through the window of the restaurant before kicking another between the legs. The remaining men's assaults seemed to do nothing to the woman as she turned her intentions upon them. Brandon shuddered and kept driving.

Brandon was about to pull into his apartment's parking lot when he noticed one of his neighbors, Mr. Zimmer. Zimmer was a man in his early 50's that liked to keep to himself, play music, and not be bothered unless he was on a walk with his dog. Yet as Brandon slowed to roll down his window and say hello, he noticed that the day's weirdness continued. At last, curiosity got the best of Brandon as he decided to see what the fuck was going on.

Mr. Zimmer, usually a refined, yet laid back sort of man, looked like he'd been rolled through garbage, then dog shit, then garbage again for good measure. His battered clothing was the least of his troubles, though. Mr. Zimmer's hair was half removed, he drooled as he walked stiffly, and dragged a bloody collar on a leash with no dog in sight. His eyes were wide as he looked about confused.

Brandon cleared his throat, keeping his car in drive just in case. "Good afternoon, Mr. Zimmer," he said as he looked over his neighbor again. "Rough day?"

Mr. Zimmer looked at him, pointing all around wildly. "Eyah, ah ah ooooh," he said. At least that is the best translation Brandon could conjure from it.

"I see," said Brandon, looking again at the empty collar and leash. "You seem to have forgot Rufus," he offered.

Mr. Zimmer became more frantic as he pointed at the collar and all around again. "Iyee oh eeh a oooo," he said.

"That bad, huh?" asked Brandon coolly. It wasn't a good idea to escalate shit in a shitstorm, so he kept as chill as he could. "Lot of crazy stuff happening today."

Mr. Zimmer then jumped up and down before pointing to his right arm. "Ayah, yah uh! Vaca ceen shit bull!"

Brandon nodded to this. "Uh huh. Yeah, that will do it for sure. You have a nice day, Mr. Z. And we will see you around," said Brandon as he drove away, still fucked up by the encounter.

Mr. Zimmer watched him go, stomping on the ground in apparent agitation. "Es iz shit bull. Shit bull!"

Pulling into his parking space, Brandon was extra cautious exiting his vehicle. He quickly made his way up into his building and door. Entering his apartment, he shut the door and pressed his back against it. The relief he felt in that moment was nigh blissful.

"Home sweet home," he whispered.

"Dude! Bro! We are so fucking glad you're here, man!"

Brandon nearly jumped out of his skin. Happy that it was just his roommate yet bummed he was not alone, Brandon eyed Josh as his friend approached him. In all honesty, Josh did not look well. His skin was pale, borderline white in fact, and his eyes had taken on a predatory glow. Josh looked about like he was seeing the apartment for the very first time, studying facets with incredible scrutiny. Brandon watched him until Josh's focus returned upon him.

"What's up, man?" asked Brandon curiously.

"I don't fucking know, bro!" bellowed Josh as he paced about. "I have been feeling funky ever since I got vaccinated today. I'm thirsty, and I'm hungry, and nothing's helping, man. We bought groceries for the week and we've already eaten them all."

"Did you guys get high? Cause that is a serious case of the munchies," mused Brandon.

"Don't I fucking wish!" Josh stopped to look at Brandon curiously. "Like, you look different to me. More detailed.

And I can smell you. Like I smell blood and coffee and the mall and M&Ms all at once. This has got me all fucked up," said Josh as he focused on Brandon's bandaged hand.

Brandon then slowly moved his injured hand back and forth, watching as Josh followed it intently. He then snapped his fingers with his uninjured hand to get his friend's attention. "Focus, Josh. Is Sarah like this too?"

Josh nodded. "Yeah. Craziest fucking thing I tell you. She's showering, hoping that it helps."

"You both had the same reaction to the vaccine," said Brandon as he pondered the situation. "Did they mention the full side effects in the brochure?"

"Fuck yeah, they did," said Josh. "But nothing like this. They told us to look out for minor irritation, allergy symptoms, shit like that. Look at my skin, man! I look like a polished cadaver."

"Josh!" screamed Sarah as she stormed into the living room. She had a towel wrapped around her body as she looked sternly at her man. Her skin too was near white, yet the changes to her skin and eyes made her more alluring. "You aren't going to believe this. My period, it's over."

"Well thanks for the TMI, babe. I am sure that is exactly what Brandon wanted to know. Though it is nice to know that sex is back on the menu," offered Josh.

Sarah looked at Brandon apologetically. "Hey, Brandon. Sorry about that," she said before she paused to stare at his bandaged hand too. Shaking her head clear she focused back on Josh. "No, you don't understand. I started last night. It's gone, completely."

Josh grinned. "Well maybe this vaccine crap isn't completely bad after all," he stated.

Sarah gave him a push. "Not funny!"

To all their surprise, Sarah's push sent Josh against the nearest wall. Josh crashed into the wall, breaking the little stand as well as going partially through the wall. He mirrored the wide-eyed look that Sarah was giving him as he pulled himself free. No one said a word as they all processed this.

"What. The. Actual. Fucking. Fuck?" Josh asked as he examined himself. "How did you do that? Why didn't it hurt at all?"

Sarah shook her head as she examined her boyfriend and the wall. "I don't know! Are you okay, baby?"

Josh nodded to her. "Fuck yeah, I'm fine!" he said as he picked up one of Aaron's game controllers on the counter. He then crushed it in his hand like it was made of paper mache. "Holy fuck, babe. I think we got superpowers!"

"That is unexpected," said Brandon as he inched slowly toward his friends. "Now for the sake of your friend and our home, please tone it down a bit."

Josh turned his head and smiled at Brandon. "Dude, this is fucking sweet."

"Wait!" said Brandon as he inched closer to Josh. "Open your mouth, Josh."

Josh shrugged. "Okay," he replied as he did as he was asked.

Now close to Josh, Brandon examined his mouth. His teeth were brilliantly white, nigh perfect in fact. And he noticed that the canines were all larger and sharper than before. Brandon then reached out and poked Josh's chest. To his surprise, it was like touching cool marble.

"Okay then," said Brandon as he slowly backed away. "I am going to try to keep my cool and not lose my shit here, but it looks like you two are fucking vampires."

"Say what?" they asked Brandon in near unison.

Brandon nodded. “Yup. Fucking vampires. I know that sounds crazy as all get out but look what just happened. Look at your teeth. This shit has just taken a sharp turn into way-out-there-land,” he said.

Brandon watched as Josh and Sarah looked at one another. They began poking each other tentatively, examining each other’s bodies and teeth. They stared long and hard, processing the information that they were receiving. Then, relaxing themselves, the two lovers offered one another a deep grin.

And then they immediately proceeded to lose their shit.

Like, completely.

Full on batshit mode.

“Holy fuckity fuck all!” screamed Josh as he ran about.

“Shit, shit, shit!” screamed Sarah as she joined him.

“Um, guys, can we enhance the calm a few notches, please and thank you,” said Brandon, keeping a distance as best as he could.

“What the fuck do we do?” Josh whined.

“How the fuck should I know?” screamed Sarah. “This is my first rodeo in this department!”

“Guys, seriously, the neighbors. The pad. Please chill,” said Brandon.

As Brandon watched, some of his friends’ erratic movements became a blur and he could not track them. This seemed to surprise them too. Josh tripped, going headfirst into the TV. Brandon cringed as the neighbor upstairs banged on his floor to indicate they were making too much noise.

“Josh, baby!” said Sarah as she rushed to her man. She too was surprised by the speed and fell, destroying the coffee table in the process.

“Wow. Security deposit is boned now,” said Brandon, placing his hands on his head, dismayed at the scene.

“I’m fine, babe, but god damn!” said Josh as he hopped to his feet. Sarah had pulled herself up in such a way that her head hit the ceiling and cracked it severely. As she landed, her towel fell off her body. She jumped upon the couch, looking about like a wild animal.

Brandon turned his head. “Oh great. And now she is naked,” he said. “Josh, you wanna do something about that?”

Josh grabbed the towel on the floor and put it around Sarah. “Here ya go, babe,” he said.

Sarah clutched to the towel as she looked at Josh with terror in her eyes. “What the fuck do we do? Are we going to die or live forever or what?”

Josh hopped nervously on his feet, checking on one of his fingers. “Babe, I don’t know. I think it has been established by now I know less than you in most instances! I don’t know what the fuck is on the fucking roster now!”

Brandon thumped his open palm on the counter as he approached his friends. “All fucking right you two, that is enough, god damnit! Now shut the fuck up and let me talk!”

With their attention claimed, Josh and Sarah silenced themselves and sulked like scolded children. It was clear they were torn between fear and excitement, and Brandon wanted to reel them in before they didn't have an apartment left. Stepping over debris, Brandon approached them, placing a hand on a shoulder of each of them. The cool marble feeling unnerved him, yet he kept a brave face on. What really troubled him was the fact that if his suspicions were correct, then blood would be required to sate them.

And THAT was what scared the ever-loving shit out of Brandon, not his friends’ sudden transformation.

"Okay, guys," started Brandon as he prepared his pep talk. "Today has been a shit show and it doesn't look to be getting any better. I’m sure you are scared and have a million questions, but I can tell you we're getting through this mess. I am here for you and I certainly won't abandon you now, okay?"

Both of them nodded as Josh spoke to Brandon softly. "We know, man."

Brandon continued. "That being said, we have some adjustments we need to make. And before we get you anywhere, I think we need to figure all that shit out. So, what I'm going to do is go out, get some supplies, and return here as quick as I can. While I am gone, I want you both to clean up as best as you can, get dressed and try to be cool. It's a jungle outside right now so the best thing you can do is keep indoors. Are we clear?"

Both nodded again. "Yes, Brandon. Thank you," said Sarah.

"Good," said Brandon as he headed for the door. "I will be back with food. We will sort it all out together. And please, I cannot stress this enough. Fucking stay here until I get back."

The couple watched Brandon as he went, murmuring their goodbyes as he closed and locked the door behind him. Both Josh and Sarah stood in silence, fixated on the details of the mess they had created. Both marveled at their powers, but also felt horrified at what they could accomplish now. The thought of their unchecked hunger now unsettled them equally.

"We are lucky we have a friend like him," said Sarah.

"That's a fucking understatement," said Joshua.

"He loves us, for sure," added Sarah.

"For reals," said Josh.

Sarah finally looked at her boyfriend. "What are we going to do, Josh? What's going to happen to us?"

Joshua shook his head as he examined himself again. "Shit, I don't know, babe. We will do what we gotta do with what we gotta do it with," he said, taking it as deep as he could go philosophically. "I guess we better stay here till B. gets back. He'll help us figure this all out."

It was then that a heavy knock came upon their door. The two lovers jumped before composing themselves. Inching toward the door, Joshua looked through the peep hole as Sarah joined him. Josh then smelled the air as he noticed who was out there. Growling, he looked at Sarah with disdain sprawled unapologetically upon his face.

"It's our upstairs neighbor," offered Josh through clenched teeth. "I suppose he has something to say about the noise. Again. As always."

"Open the door," said Sarah with a slowly dawning smile.

"Brandon said we shouldn't leave, babe," whispered Josh.

"But he never said anything about entertaining guests," countered Sarah.

Josh grinned at this. "God dammit, you're right," he replied.

Still grinning ear to ear, Josh flung the door open and he and Sarah cast their eyes upon Jordan Anderson. Jordan was a late-thirties man of some self-importance. Jordan was a coffee sipping, glasses wearing, activist wannabe who got by mostly on his mommy and daddy's allowance. Since day one he had been a bane on the ass of Josh and Sarah's existence and had reported them on at least 12 different occasions. Suffice to say, they knew Jordan and loved him as much as a case of searing hemorrhoids. "Jordan, you smug face son of a bitch! What do we owe the pleasure?" asked Josh.

Jordan's eyes were bulging as he pointed at the couple. "You know damn well why I'm here! What the shit are you two doing down here? It's shaking my whole god damn apartment!"

Josh grinned, replying nonchalantly. "Well you know how it is, man. Them later chapters in the Karma Sutra are hardcore to the max. Lesson learned though. We could let you borrow the book if you want. I mean, if anyone needs to get laid it's you."

Jordan about lost it then. "I have had it with the both of you! Just you wait until the super hears about this," he fumed as he looked over Josh's shoulder into the apartment. "Good lord, man! Were you hosting Ultimate Fighting tryouts? Is this a domestic dispute? What in god's name are you doing in there?"

"He's seen too much," said Sarah darkly.

"Not yet, babe," offered Josh.

"This is the last time I will be visiting, you ingrates," said Jordan as he motioned to the direction of the office. "Once I report this mayhem, you are as good as gone, do you hear me? And I will laugh and rejoice your eviction for months on end and won't lose a wink of fucking sleep, do you hear me, you god damn menaces to society!"

Josh turned to look at Sarah. "Babe?" he asked.

"Certainly," said Sarah as she dropped her towel to reveal her curvaceous beauty.

Jordan's fury subsided as his eyes panned down to the naked glory before him. Suddenly it was not just his eyes that were bulging. "And I'll have you know I'm...I'm...just gonna...stand here...staring cause...cause...great googa mooga," he uttered.

Josh smiled triumphantly. "There. NOW he's seen too much," he said before grabbing Jordan by his collar and dragging his ass inside before shutting the door of the apartment.

It would be best to just glaze over the sounds that followed.

6

A SORTA SUPERHERO ORIGIN

Now vaccinated, Aaron ventured back into the food court. His arm hurt like the dickens, as the nurse administered the vaccine coarsely. It didn't help that when she asked if he preferred left or right, he offered up his butt cheeks with a wink. It took all of three minutes for the lady to be tired of his shit, and now Aaron's left arm was suffering for it.

Aaron ordered some fries and a soda before sitting down to take his time consuming them. If things got too bad, David would call or find him. If they got really bad, then he would hear his boss fuming at the top of his lungs. Aaron knew he had to get something in his stomach first. He had never been keen on vaccines, and truth be told, he was feeling just a little off after the injection.

Nibbling on his fries, Aaron half-heartedly watched the mall patrons come and go. Some of the customers gave notice and scowled at him. Others paid him no mind, okay to look over his antics because he made a damn fine slice of za. But mostly, he kept his eyes out for Shawna, hoping to see her again before he was pulled back to work. Fat chance of that though, for if anyone knew Aaron, it was Shawna.

And there was no way in hell she was going to let lightning strike twice in one day, no sir. Now good day.

As Aaron munched, he was soon offered company in the form of David. Wordless his partner in pain sat down and helped himself to a handful of fries. Aaron watched David as he surveyed the food court, fixing his gaze upon what he affectionally called "the mamacitas." You see, David held no shame in his quest for love. Most women caught him checking them out. And when they did, that is when he really turned it up a notch.

"And he's on the hunt," offered Aaron between bites.

David nodded astutely. "Yeah, man. It's hard to find women who can keep up with a much lover," said David. That's pronounced Da-veed by the way. This has been covered previously.

"I bet," said Aaron as he followed David's gaze. "Has the crafty predator singled out its prey yet?" he asked.

"Yeah, man," said David as he pointed. "I think it's time Janette got to know the real David."

"Look, David," started Aaron.

"Da-veed," said David.

"That's again what I said," said Aaron, pressing on. "Janette is a fine ass conquest I assure you, but no way in hell she is dating someone from work. She doesn't do that anymore."

"And how do you know that?" asked David.

"Cause I am the reason she made that rule," said Aaron, holding up some fries in a toast.

David shook his head. "Maybe it doesn't work with you, but I am David. David works for all women," he mused.

“I will give you this, my friend,” mused Aaron to David. “Your confidence and denial skills are fucking outstanding,” He then motioned back to the deli. Hold the fort a bit longer. I’m almost back from my break.”

“I don’t know, man. The view’s nice today. I think it’s a good time for a break,” said David with a grin.

“What do you want?”

David leaned in. “I don’t know. Maybe Janette’s number and you putting in good words for the much lover,” he said.

“I can try,” said Aaron. “But she might not like any good words from me. And I can guarantee you that your chances are fucked if I use anything remotely close to ‘much lover.’”

David leaned casually back in his chair, scoping at the scene in the food court with deliberate nonchalance. “Then maybe David will stay right here, take a long break like lazy gringos and find the mamacitas for himself,” he said.

Aaron finally held up his hands in defeat. “Alright, alright. I’ll see what I can do. Just don’t fuck it up too much. If shit goes south, I don’t want in the crossfire. I just only recently gotten things out of the hostility phase and I’d like to keep it that way,” he said.

“When you please women like David does, no woman can be hostile to you,” said David.

“Go hold the fort, Don Juan. I’ll see you in a minute.”

“You got it, man,” said David with a triumphant grin. Aaron watched him go, shaking his head. He loved that sumbitch David. Great guy to hang, drink, and work with, but when it came to David, Aaron was damn glad he wasn’t a woman.

Still musing to himself, Aaron continued eating his fries. He was feeling a bit better after consuming the greasy goodness but wasn’t ready to return to work just yet. He didn’t know if it was due to the vaccine or just giving no free fucks about his job, but either way he was more content to sit. As he finished the last of his snack, he crumpled up the container to a ball and casually tossed it toward the trash, a shot he'd made many times over.

"Shit," he breathed, knowing his aim was off. He held out his hand, wishing for a redo, willing it to not hit the floor.

And, just like that, the shot redirected and hit the trash perfectly.

"What the fucks, what?" said Aaron as he looked about, wondering if he was crazy or being fucked with somehow. No one was watching him. No one had seen the trash realign to make it into the waste receptacle. Aaron wondered if he was losing his shit, or if the vaccine had boned him up more than he realized. Sitting back in his chair, he processed this new information.

Aaron looked about again, needing desperately to know if he had lost it or not. If he didn't figure it out, the lack of such knowledge would drive him bonkers. Aaron looked down at the table, seeing the unused ketchup packet he had left. Sure that no one he knew was approaching, Aaron held out his hand, focusing on the packet. He willed it to move, gently, softly, for he didn't want to cause a stir. Nothing happened, so he pressed a bit harder, hoping for even a little tremble.

But nope, that's not how it happened.

Just as Aaron was about to give up hope, the ketchup packet exceeded his expectations by a whole hell of a lot. His little mental "push" sent the packet shooting like a bullet across the food court. Aaron gawked as it hit the back of a customer's head. The man felt the back of his skull and screamed upon seeing red, fearing he had been shot. Realizing it was ketchup, he turned to the gentleman standing behind him and pushed him fiercely. A scuffle then broke out as two of the janitors rushed over to deal with it.

Aaron looked at his hands in disbelief and soon was lost in the revelation and possibility. “Holy sheep shit on a raincoat. I’ve got superpowers,” he whispered, wanting to jump the fuck up and down but smart enough to keep his composure in the food court.

Keeping quiet and still, Aaron looked about. He had to test this further while also ensuring it wasn’t some fluke. Aaron took a few deep breaths, wanting nothing but complete focus. This was when his years as a devout gamer fixated on a screen was going to finally pay off.

Aaron decided to start off small. Reaching into his pocket he procured his Tic-Tacs, pouring out the remainder of the pack in his hand. Counting, he had nine left. Putting one of these in his right hand, he searched about the food court for a proper target for his experiment. It didn’t take long for him to find the douche from before, hailing from Chicago. By the look on the lady behind the counter’s face, he was making another impossible request as he looked quite animated talking to her.

Aaron smiled wickedly as he focused on the Tic-Tac. Channeling his will, he sent the Tic-Tac hurtling forward like a pellet. The Tic-Tac struck his target on the ass, making him scream out as he startled the cashier. Grabbing at his wounded butt cheek, he looked about confused. With no one near him, he turned back to the cashier and resumed his impossible request.

“This is not going to be your day, bub,” said Aaron as he procured another Tic-Tac, aimed, and fired upon the left cheek this time.

Screaming out again, the agitated cashier told him to keep it down or she would refuse service to him. The man raised his voice, now holding to both of his buttocks in an angry, pained tirade. Aaron procured two more minty pieces of ammo and set up his aim. Firing again, he struck the man's hands. The man wailed as he slammed his hands on the counter and hopped up and down, shaking his wounded appendages. The cashier demanded that the man leave. The man vowed to return before turning and looking about suspiciously.

And as he did, Aaron fired again. This Tic Tac hit the man in the crotch, causing him to leap first and then land on his knees. He cried in his pain and confusion as he laid his back on the counter wall behind him. Aaron saw it as an opportunity to press the issue. He tilted the hot sauce sitting on the counter over, letting it fall on the man's head.

Once the hot sauce bypassed the man's hair and hit his eyes, he clutched at them as he wailed once more. The man clamored to his feet, frantic to wash his eyes clean and be free of the cursed mall he found himself in. Standing again, the man ran wildly grasping his face. He barreled over three customers before running face first into a wall and knocking himself unconscious. Aaron clenched his teeth, trying not to laugh out loud so that he could continue his "research."

The next five minutes or so were in fact a blur of glorious amusement for Aaron as his antics escalated. He popped a candy bar off a shelf at the snack shop and had it travel across the floor to him. He made one of the fountain drink machines go completely batshit. A couple of well deserving "regulars" ended up wearing their food and drinks. It was a regular symphony of mischief that had the food court awash in calamity as Aaron enjoyed his Snickers, perhaps the most satisfying Snickers of his life.

"There you are, motherfucker!"

Aaron almost jumped out of his seat, for instinctively he knew someone was talking to him. He turned in time to see an unfortunately familiar, great big asshole storming toward him.

Immediately he recognized him as Matt Dillonsworth, Shawna's current boyfriend. The insecure male of a jock, upon starting his courtship with Shawna, immediately hated Aaron for no other reason than he was Shawna's ex-boyfriend.

Of course, the stories Matt had heard over time didn't help the matter either.

Matt came to the other side of the table, upturning the chair there for emphasis before he slamming both hands down. Aaron picked up his drink to save it from the assault as he watched Matt curiously. Matt was unofficially the poster boy for the "Bro, do you even lift" movement. Proud of his workouts and body, Matt affirmed this with an unhealthy number of selfies on social media. He, of course, worked at the health store where he could unleash his health-minded doctrines and supplements on the local populace.

Taking a moment to stare angrily at Aaron, Matt tried to let his silence intimidate Aaron further. Aaron sat back, sipping his soda casually and giving no fucks, which made Matt all the angrier. Aaron found it funnier still, cause obviously the wheels in Matt's head needed lube. And so, Aaron waited, anxious to see where this went with his newfound powers and all.

"I can tell by how Shawna's acting that you talked to her. I thought I fucking told you to stay away from my woman," barked Matt.

Taking on the voice of the Hulk, Aaron did a pretty solid parody of Shawna's man. "Matt no like you talk to girl. Hurt's Matt's feelings. Matt smash!"

Matt threw a finger in Aaron's face. "You won't find it so funny when I teach you a god damn lesson," he roared.

"Matt use rage, compensate for small pee-pee," said Aaron, still using a silly Hulk voice.

"I am gonna slap that fucking look off your face, asswipe," spat Matt.

Aaron shook his head. "So I bumped into her. I tried to say hello, even. It's not like we are fucking or something. Are you that insecure? I mean it would explain the overabundance of muscles."

Matt looked away, smiling as he kept his composure. "You get one more chance. You talk to Shawna again and I will fucking end you. So, all you gotta do is tell me you are going to keep clear of her and we're cool. And trust me, you want to keep things cool between us," he said.

"You know this is absolutely ridiculous," started Aaron. "You doing this right now, putting on this silly ass show? Yeah, it's ridiculous. And you know what? I'm tired of it. And the best part about it? I can say that now and don't have to give a lab rat's ass what you think about it."

"Is that so?" asked Matt.

"That is so," said Aaron before resuming his Hulk voice. "If Matt no like it then Matt can fuck the fuck off."

"That's it," said Matt as he raised his fist to clock Aaron from across the table.

The muscle fueled fist came soaring at Aaron yet stopped as suddenly as it started. It then just hovered there, trembling as Matt stared at it in amazement. Matt looked between his frozen fist and Aaron, who was now grinning ear to ear. Aaron then motioned with his hand and Matt's first redirected and struck Matt across the jaw twice. Matt fell to his knees before his fist went behind his head and smashed his face onto the table. Matt gazed at Aaron as if the gods were smiting him while people began to stare.

Aaron waved to those watching. "Sorry, folks, he's having a rough go. It's not every day you have to accept you have a small dong," he said before focusing back on Matt. "Do I have your attention yet?"

"I am gonna fucking kill you," growled Matt as he tried to stand up.

"I find this lack of faith…disturbing," said Aaron as he held out a hand before him and made a squeezing motion.

As Aaron made the movement with his hand, Matt gasped and made a shrill cry as pressure mounted between his legs. "My balls…my balls," he croaked.

"Now do I have your attention, or do I squeeze just a wee bit more?"

"We cool, we cool!" breathed Matt painfully.

"I thought so. Glad you could see things my way," said Aaron as he kicked his feet on the table. "Look, Matt. I don't know what the fuck is going on here or why or how I can do this. My guess is it had something to do with the vaccine. Point is, I am tired of your shit and won't be taking your macho dick swagger no more. Are we clear, sunshine?"

"She's my girl, fucker," said Matt defiantly.

"I see we are still failing to communicate on a deeper, more profound level," said Aaron as he motioned with his free hand again. This time, Matt's other hand went down the back of his pants. Matt gasped and whined as he gave himself a prostate exam. "Now Matt, apparently I could do this all day, but I don't know how much of this you are going to be able to take. But the more you talk shit the more I am forced to make you look like a total asshat."

"Fuck you," breathed Matt as he tried to stand again. Aaron motioned again, and the exam threatened to probe deeper. The large man planted his face on the table in defeat.

Satisfied that he had Matt's full attention, Aaron continued. "So here's how it's going to be, Matt. We are going to go about our lives and take things as they come. If

Shawna talks to me, she talks to me. If she doesn't, she doesn't. But these things aren't going to be marred by you being an insecure twat waffle. And if you try any of this shit again, all I can promise is that whatever I do to you will be worse than what you are feeling right now," he said.

"How can this get any god damn worse?" asked Matt.

Aaron leaned in closer, smiling. "You really want to find that out? I mean, I bet with a lot of pain and manipulation we can put a new meaning to me telling you to go fuck yourself," he said gleefully.

"Alright. Alright," breathed Matt in defeat. "We're cool. Truce. Can I fucking go now, asshole?"

Aaron offered a pained, sympathetic expression. "You see, that's the thing, Matt. When you say things like that, it just screams to me that you are carrying some repressed anger and would only try to get revenge if I let you go," he said as he held up his fist to make a squeezing motion again. "Perhaps I need to help you come to grips with reality a bit more."

Matt shook his head furiously. "No! We're good man. Cool as cool, Right as fucking rain, I swear. Now please let my nuts alone and get this finger out of my ass!" He said these things louder than he wanted and more people cast curious eyes at him.

Aaron again looked at the those watching. "He'll be okay. We are working on his anger issues," he said before smiling again at Matt. "So I think we are just about done here. But there is just one more thing I have to do to get my point across."

"What are you going to do?" whined Matt.

"I am going to tell you a joke, a really bad joke. And you won't like it." Aaron said.

"Okay," said Matt suspiciously.

"So Matt," started Aaron with a grin. "What kind of tea is the hardest to swallow in the world?"

"I so give up," said Matt.

"Reality, Matt. Definitely reality," he said as he motioned again with his hand. Matt's hand came up from his pants. As it exited, Matt breathed a sigh of pure relief. "Now I don't know about you, but I think that one was facepalm worthy."

"What does that, OH, GOD, NO!" Matt cried.

But it was too late cause Aaron had already offered an involuntary assist.

Thoroughly humiliated, Matt bolted toward the bathroom, wiping at his face, spitting, and gagging as he did so. Aaron watched him go, while clearly pleased. People who had been watching the weird ass situation went about their business, shaking their heads and mumbling their judgements. Aaron was all too happy to wave at them as they passed by.

"I should leave him alone," said Aaron as he stood and stretched. He then shrugged with a grin. "But I can't," he added before heading happily toward the men's room.

With both Aaron and Matt gone, the food court slowly resumed to being close to normal once more. But within minutes there was another scream as the men's room door flew open. Matt emerged, his face covered in soap, his entire back covered in toilet water as he hopped out of the bathroom with his pants around his ankles. He made it several feet before he fell to the ground. Not wasting any time, he proceeded to inch across the floor like a deranged, drunk caterpillar.

As the crowd watched in horror, Aaron emerged from the bathroom whistling. From across the food court he caught sight of David looking for him. As they made eye contact, he gave his friend a thumbs up.

"David!" called out Aaron jubilantly. And yes he said it right. "I think I am going to call it a day, man. Tell Bob I seemed to have left all my fucks at home and I am going to go see if I can find them."

David watched as Aaron happily ventured toward the mall's exit. "Aye, mi amigo," he said, shaking his head. "Pinche loco."

But then David was distracted by a group of mamacitas and all was forgiven and forgotten as far as he was concerned.

7

AND JESUS WEPT, CAUSE ALL THIS SUCKED

Detective Raymond Weller looked grimly at the monitor linked to the camera in the interrogation room. He had read the preliminary report and talked to the officers present, but this was still pretty batshit to him. The last few weeks had been an ever-growing shit storm of calamity, but this took the taco. And so Detective Weller stared intently at the bloodied, robe toting, sandal sporting, mess of a man that now sat somberly at a little table waiting for judgment.

Detective Weller was a career man, twenty years into the department and the stress had definitely gotten to him. He was grateful to still have most his hair, but the crap he had seen on the job had grayed it prematurely. He kept an appropriate amount of hair stubble upon his face, mostly because it beat shaving. His blue eyes were calculating wells of serious cynicism. Many still considering him a striking man in his grey suit and tie, but he knew those days would come to an end soon. After all, nature was a cruel and fickle mistress.

The last few weeks had gone to great lengths to give Weller an ulcer. Crime was at an all-time high. Riots, parties, and orgies broke out frequently these days and at a moment's notice and often hand in hand. With the supposed pending end of the world looming, people were quick to cash in their last fuck and party like it was 1999, if you dig Prince and all.

And if you don't well you likely have made more than doves cry in your lifetime.

Detective Weller kept his intentness upon the monitor. Two officers who had been on scene stood close by, prepared to talk but loathe to do so. Weller didn't know if their recollections would help him grasp the insanity that plagued him. Answers were what he craved and certainty were a rare and dwindling commodity of late.

The only certainty that he could hold on to these days was the fact that, like Detective Murtaugh, he was too old for this shit.

Detective Weller took one more look at the file in his hands and the monitor before he began musing. "So, this is our John Doe," he said absently to the fidgeting officers that shared the room with him.

"It's fucking Jesus, sir," said the younger of the two officers.

"Which you clearly stated in your report," answered Weller casually.

"Never seen anything like it before," said the older, taller officer. "Fish and wine flying everywhere. I tell you, that son of a bitch wields a mean mackerel."

"I see," said Detective Weller before he turned to look upon Officers Wagner and Creasy. The duo together looked like the shitty reboot of Andy Taylor and Barney Fife straight out of modern-day Mayberry. Both officers appeared frazzled, exhausted, and covered in fish guts. In fact, the smell was starting to permeate the room. "And you guys are convinced this is in fact Jesus?"

Officer Wagner shrugged. He was the seasoned and more practical of the two. "I don't know about all of that, sir, but he's not rightly human. We had fish falling from the sky. Creasy's trigger happy ass shot him once and he healed it before knocking the snot out of Creasy with a halibut. Hell, Officer Pensky's still in the bathroom crapping fish eggs as we speak. It was the damndest thing any of us have ever seen."

"And how many cops were on the scene?" asked the detective.

"15 all together," said Officer Wagner. "And damned if it wasn't enough to stop him. We struck, tazed, maced, and even shot that guy, detective, and nothing stopped him. Think we only pissed him off. I am just glad he had some restraint. I can't imagine being like Pensky shitting caviar till I am blue in the face."

"And how did you finally subdue the perpetrator?" inquired Weller.

Creasy chimed in. "Officer Wagner brought him a coffee."

"I see," said the detective.

"Yeah, that calmed him down," Officer Wagner confirmed. "That's actually how our altercation started thanks to Officer Triggerhappy here."

"It was a reflex!" whined Creasy.

"You have been dying for an excuse to shoot that thing," countered Wagner before diverting his attention back to Detective Weller. "Like I was saying, he calmed down and came quietly after that."

"Not quite," said Creasy.

"How do you mean?" asked Weller.

"Oh yeah, right," said Officer Wagner. "Yeah, he felt bad, so he healed everyone first. Every scratch, cut, and bruise. Save for the fish eggs in Officer Pensky's ass. He said Pensky still deserved those."

"Well he is kind of a dick," said Creasy.

"I can't argue there," said Wagner.

"There's always been something about that guy. Leave it to Jesus to see it," said Creasy.

"That could be a show right there. Forget the Beaver, I'd watch Leave it to Jesus," said Officer Wagner.

"That's enough, already," said Detective Weller, growing annoyed with the banter. "I think I got all I need here, you two are dismissed for the moment."

The two officers excused themselves from the room, still talking about the proposed show as Detective Weller felt his ulcer say hello. Weller spent a few more moments reviewing the file and watching the screen. There was something to all this that didn't sit well, like some foreboding feeling of gloom and doom. He hadn't felt such a feeling since walking down the aisle. Weller didn't listen to his gut then, but he was sure as shit going to listen to it now.

Entering the interrogation room, Officer Weller observed as the lone occupant looked up to watch him. The resemblance and ensemble were uncanny, from the tattered robes and sandals to the scars on his hands. There was a pain in the man's eyes that was undeniable, and Weller felt sympathy he chose to hide under a bad cop image. The man waited for Officer Weller as he sat himself on the opposite side of the table, still looking over the file.

"Christ, Jesus H.," started Officer Weller before looking up. "You've had yourself one hell of a day it seems."

The one called Jesus nodded. "More than you can possibly fathom, my child," he said somberly. "The world has become unmanageable."

Officer Weller watched his suspect with the utmost scrutiny. "Some officers of the precinct seem to think you are the real thing, come back for a second coming if you will. What do you have to say to that?"

The one called Jesus looked at him, holding nothing back in emotion. "Does it matter to you, my son? I felt the world needed me more than ever, yet I can see now that my lessons are lost, that the message of love has been overturned. There was nothing for me in a house of God. And to my shame, for the first time in centuries, I lost my temper."

"Not the actions of a supreme being," offered Weller.

Jesus shook his head. "Indeed not. But you must understand in this form I am made flesh, so despite my powers, I feel what you feel, including anger. The floodgate could only hold it back for so long."

Detective Weller motioned to the whole of Jesus. "I gotta admit. It's a great act. I bet you would be a hit in the cosplay circles and cons. But the jig's up. You are facing multiple accounts of assault, trespassing, destruction of private property, and resisting arrest. Hell, ICE wants to have some words with you since you cannot provide documentation of citizenship. Why don't you drop the charade and tell us who you really are. We can't help you if you don't help us."

Jesus smiled at him sadly. "You still do not believe, do you?" he observed.

"I believe you are a brilliant illusionist and perhaps a conman, but nothing beyond that," replied Weller.

"Then what is it going to take, my child?" asked Jesus in earnest. "Must I walk on water yet again? Alter your beverage? Do you require healing of some sort?"

Detective Weller put the file upon the table as he crossed his hands. "No parlor tricks are going to change the fact of what you did," he said.

Jesus nodded. "I am not asking for forgiveness. I simply want you to believe," he said.

"I hear you have a knack for conjuring sushi," said the detective chuckling.

Jesus nodded. "Oh yes," he replied before putting his hands at his waist and bringing them back up holding the tail of a ten-pound salmon. He slapped the fish upon the table before conjuring a mackerel, tuna, and a handful of minnows. "I assume this will help since I was thoroughly inspected for weapons upon my arrival."

Detective Weller stood quickly, backing away from the table and knocking over his chair. "How in the fuck did you do that?" he demanded.

Jesus shook his head. "I have always been able to conjure food for my flock. I mean, it is in the bible after all. One of the things that was not wrought with alterations and false interpretations," he said before motioning to the table. "Shall I produce more for you?"

Detective Weller shook his head, still trying to take in the trick he had just seen. "No, I think this police station has seen enough fish for one lifetime, thank you," he said. "How did you do that, where were you hiding those fish?"

"I do not think I favor what you are likely implying," said Jesus.

The detective regained his resolve, clinching his fists as he crossed his arms. "So, what's your angle? Are you going to lawyer up on me now? Try to get off on insanity?"

Jesus shook his head. "Oh no, my son. I am guilty. I who am without sin have sinned. That I cannot deny. But it is I who should warn you. If I am left contained, this world will see a wrath the likes that have never seen before."

"Is that a threat?"

Jesus looked hurt at the accusation. "Not at all, my child. I simply mean that I need to be out there protecting my children. I am too late to stop the horrors that are coming."

"And what horrors are those?" demanded the detective.

Jesus's tone became severe. "Mankind has meddled in powers it cannot comprehend, my son. It has discovered an ancient resting place and extracted from it an untold power. It is the basis used in what you call a vaccine…Omega as they call it…and soon you will see the perils of such misguided steps."

"What, are you a prophet now too?" chided the detective.

Jesus offered him a wry, pained smile. "There are a few out there that would call me that, yes," he said.

"I think you are pretty close to being the lock-him-up-and-throw-away-the-fucking-key guy," offered Detective Weller.

"I am here because I choose to be, my son," said Jesus.

"Ugh!" spat the detective disgustedly. "Enough of that shit already."

The Jesus man was not swayed but such frustration. "You look stressed, my son. That will do you no good. If you brought water, I could conjure you a soothing and healing elixir," he said.

Detective Weller held up his hands, shaking his head. "Oh, I don't think so, buddy. I have seen enough crazy shit today, thank you," he said.

Suddenly both the detective and Jesus were drawn to a sharp rapping on the door. Cracking the door, Officer Wagner stuck his head in the room as he looked quite stricken. "Detective Weller, you might want to have a look at this. It's bad. Really bad," he said before shutting the door and rushing away.

"I will never say I told you so, but it lingers in the air silently regardless," offered Jesus.

Detective Weller fought the urge to reach across the table and bless Jesus with a proverbial bitch slap. Instead he pointed a shaky finger at him. "You just sit tight. I will be back to deal with you soon enough." He then stormed to the door. "Fuck I need a drink," he added.

"I offered," said Jesus.

"Shut the hell up!" screamed Weller.

Adam, the man Jesus, watched as the door was slammed harshly. He could hear the commotion outside, for calamity was now surely ensuing. Adam knew that this was the beginning and that it would only grow worse. Lowering his head, he thought on such things and his purpose in such an environment.

"I must do what I must, regardless of the outcome," he whispered.

Adam then broke the chain of the handcuffs that held him. He then placed a finger on both cuffs, and they opened mystically. Standing, he prepared himself for things to come. Grabbing the salmon on the table, Adam slung it over his shoulder as he looked at the door.

"And so it begins, the end," he whispered before heading out of the interrogation room and onto further adventures.

8

THE ASSHOLE

Douglas Whitworth sat lazily in his luxurious chair, watching the camera feeds he had stationed across his mall with hungry eyes. Mr. Whitworth had taken ownership of the Cedar Park Mall upon his father's death ten years prior, grateful for the chance and the inheritance waiting for him upon his dad's demise. Instantly, Mr. Whitworth, as he liked to always be called, implemented changes to maximize profits, filter clientele, and forge the mall into his vision of a money-making engine.

Leaning back in his chair, Douglas observed intently as he patted his profoundly spoiled belly. Strangers would deem him overweight, people that knew him deemed him a fat fuck of a man, but both categories were beneath Mr. Whitworth as far as he was concerned. His balding head was strategically covered with what hair that remained and fixed in place with oodles of hairspray. It was a hairdo that fooled no one, but bolstered his ego nonetheless. His sausage-like fingers rapped upon his wrinkled yet obscenely expensive suit as he decided his next step.

Mr. Whitworth was ready for phase two of his grand scheme, yet his mall was still littered with holdouts. He wanted nothing less than the upper crust, not the mallrats or riffraff that still trickled into what he called "his house." Mr. Whitworth would keep raising rent and standards until only the elite remained. Then his vision would be all but complete and the money would flow like salmon during spawning season.

It was great to be rich and important.

Taking a moment to peel his eyes from his slew of monitors, Douglas looked upon his lavish and grotesquely spacious office. Every necessity required was catered in glorious fashion, including the opulent snack trolley, fully stocked bar, and a side room with a bed. The bed was there for frequent naps as well as "intense negotiations" he had with desperate or paid for women. (Truth be told, they were often both) Pictures with celebrities and politicians littered his walls as well as mock awards, articles and tributes to himself. This was Douglas's throne room and here he felt like the god he knew that he was.

Satisfied with the grand vision that was his office, Douglas returned his focus to his monitors. Here he observed who entered his mall, what needed dealt with, and women that might be in need of his "services." Douglas made mental notes for later, including addressing employees that needed release. A score of the custodians were on top of the list.

Douglas stood then to fetch a drink, giving his chair relief from his nearly 300-pound girth. He then thought better of the endeavor and sat back down, calling in his secretary to fetch it for him. Douglas watched the shapely blonde twenty-something pour him his scotch on the rocks intently, admiring his newest employee's curves. Soon they would sit to discuss her future at the mall and just how bad she wanted that raise.

Accepting his beverage, Douglas watched his secretary leave, hiding nothing in his lustful gazes. The secretary shivered and shut the door to his office. Douglas had a mind to berate her if he could remember her name. They would sort it all out later in the negotiations room. Should negotiations fail, Douglas would simply replace her with a secretary who understood and embraced his "policies."

Hell, he was going to do that eventually anyway.

It was not long before there came a knock at the door. The door opened softly, revealing Robin Simmons, Mr. Whitworth's personal assistant. Mr. Simmons had been Douglas's right-hand man for roughly five years. Thin, refined, and sophisticatedly sharp dressed, Robin was the anti-Douglas in terms of appearance, and as cleanly as he appeared, the man had no qualms about burying his nose up his boss's ass.

Robin entered, carrying multiple bags that consisted of Mr. Douglas's lunch. Mr. Douglas waited patiently as Robin placed the bags down and brought forth said lunch, setting it out for Mr. Douglas and placing a bib upon him. Robin carried this duty out like it was second nature, resembling a parent about to feed their child. Mr. Douglas looked upon the spread which consisted of lobster, shrimp scampi, a steak, garlic mashed potatoes, burger, and a side salad with dressing on the side.

Observing the contents of a meal forged from multiple restaurants, Mr. Douglas looked at Robin disappointedly. "I see the pizza is missing," he observed.

Robin nodded. "It is, sir, but sadly out of my control. Runsky's was closed today for some reason," he offered apologetically. “A definite shame to discover especially since it is nearly ten miles away.”

“Well I suppose you did your best,” said Mr. Douglas as he started in on his scampi. “Did you get the vaccine?”

Robin came around the desk, helping Mr. Whitworth out of his jacket and rolling up his sleeves as Whitworth continued to eat. “Of course, though it was not without cost. It would have been easier had you just went and got it done,” said Robin.

“What’s money if such inconveniences cannot be avoided?” said Douglas between bites.

“I wouldn’t know,” said Robin as he fetched the vaccine. “You know you could always let me fetch you pizza from downstairs.”

Douglas practically choked on his lobster. “I won’t be eating anything else from that hellhole, not with that snot nosed punk they have working there,” he spat.

Robin nodded as he prepped the vaccine to be administered. “Ah, yes. Aaron. He’s not too keen on special requests.”

“His days at my mall are numbered,” said Douglas as he opened his Diet Coke and drained half the can. “Now hurry up with the vaccine already. I want to be done with it.”

“Of course, sir,” said Robin as he brought over a syringe full of the Omega vaccine.

As Robin prepped his arm with an alcohol swab, Douglas spoke to him through bites. “I think it may be time for the secretary’s annual review, if you draw my meaning,” he said.

“I unfortunately do,” said Robin with a sigh. “You keep going through receptionist this quickly and you are going to garner a reputation.”

Douglas was unperturbed by this. "Turnaround is a healthy part of a thriving business," he said between large bites. "Besides, this one hasn't displayed any type of loyalty yet."

"Well, Sandra is still new," observed Robin.

"No excuse. She has yet to show she is willing to be a valued member of our team and we can't have that," said Douglas.

"I'll schedule the review," said Robin as he held the syringe at the ready. "But first I will stick you before you try to stick her, so to speak."

"That a boy," said Douglas before he yelped. "Shit, Robin! Fucking be careful with the needle. You fucking hurt me!"

"Terribly sorry, sir. Smallest needle they had," said Robin as he discarded the needle and swab. "Your pain brings me no joy," he added indifferently. "But if it helps at all, I brought you a lollipop."

"It doesn't," said Douglas bitterly as he resumed eating. After long moments he looked at Robin expectantly. "Is it cherry at least?"

"Of course, sir."

"Fine. Set it on my desk," said Douglas.

Complying, Robin looked at his boss expectantly. "Will that be all, sir?" he asked.

"For now, I suppose," mumbled Douglas as he looked around his desk. "Did you forget the ketchup?"

Robin shook his head. "Not at all, sir," he offered before reaching in the leftover bag on the desk and procuring the request.

"Then I guess that's all," said Douglas indifferently. "But keep close."

"As you wish," said Robin as he exited the office.

Now free, Robin let his façade fall and breathed in the fresh air of momentary freedom. Catering to such a diva was exhausting, regardless of the payout. Now certain his boss was fully engaged in his lunch, Robin offered a wry grin to Sandra who returned the smile. Robin strutted over and sat on the edge of her desk. He'd give his boss almost everything there was, but this new gal was his.

"I swear, I don't know how you put up with him," said Sandra as she gushed at Robin.

"It's a talent I have for survival I suppose," said Robin as he adjusted his glasses and winked at her. "Though you best be on your guard. He's looking to 'negotiate' with you soon, if you catch my drift."

"Ugh," choked Sandra with a shudder. "I think I'd sooner dry hump a chainsaw."

"You would likely find more pleasure from it," offered Robin as the two of them laughed. "Seriously though. I'm not kidding. I've seen many a woman come and go that were unhappily 'negotiated.' I don't even think he believes a female orgasm is a real thing. I mean, not that he would care if he did."

"Again, how do you put up with him?"

Robin shrugged. "I am paid well to do so. Plus, I'm not a woman, and that goes a long way when dealing with him," he replied.

"So, you get some leniency then?"

Robin shrugged. "Well if I screw up, I'm still fucked, just not in the same way as you," he said.

Just then, the intercom clicked in. "Hey, um, yeah you," said Douglas over it. "Is Robin out there?"

Sandra rolled her eyes and put on her happy voice. "Yes, he is, Mr. Whitworth. Shall I send him back in to you?"

"Yes," said Mr. Whitworth. "And thank you…you."

Sandra turned off the intercom. "Looks like you are not out of the fire yet," she giggled.

"That fucker still can't be hungry," he said, rolling his eyes before he grinned once more at Sandra. "Well, if you would excuse me," he said before heading back into his boss's office.

Robin entered quietly and closed the door before turning to look at his office. He gasped as he did, for Mr. Whitworth didn't look quite like himself. The man had grown decidedly pale as he stared at his hands. Robin wondered if he had an allergic reaction to the vaccine as he rushed to Mr. Whitworth's side. "Mr. Whitworth are you alright?" asked Robin as he felt his boss's head. The man felt stone cold to the touch. "You don't look so well."

Mr. Whitworth continued to look at his hands. "It's a funny thing, really," he started as he continued to look fascinated. "I feel changed somehow, but for the better. I was scared at first, but it passed. Somehow, I feel stronger than before, sharper in fact."

Robin offered a smile. "That is a relief then, sir," he said as he motioned for the door. "Can I get you anything?"

Mr. Whitworth shook his head absently. "No, I don't believe you can," he replied as he looked at his finished meal on his desk. Whitworth had cleaned his plates completely. "But I did just discover something that I found entirely surprising," he added.

"And what's that, sir?"

Suddenly, Mr. Whitworth grabbed Robin by the wrist and pulled him on the desk with great strength. Robin tried to struggle, but the power that his boss held was far too great. He kicked and fought as Mr. Whitworth placed a hand over his mouth. He was helpless as his boss watched him intently. "You see, Robin, this fucker is in fact still very much hungry," he offered. Mr. Whitworth then threw his head back, exposing the fangs now in his mouth before sinking his teeth into the neck of his assistant.

Robin felt the piercing of his flesh as he tried to scream out in pure terror. He thrashed as the life was sucked from him hungrily. Mr. Whitworth feasted on him as ravenously as he had his lunch moments before. Soon, Robin's strength waned as his boss fucked him over one last time. Holding up a shaky hand, Robin finally told Mr. Whitworth how he truly felt with a defiant middle finger. Then, as the blood was nearly drained from him, Robin went limp and died.

Drawing his head back, Mr. Whitworth felt an amazing surge of warmth and strength wash through him. He was invigorated by the process, yet he wanted more. Something about killing and feeding had triggered something in him. His lackey had been powerless to stop him and his new strength. Mr. Whitworth looked at his arm where he had just been vaccinated, realizing that he had been bestowed a tremendous gift.

Smiling, he activated the intercom again. "Sandra, would you mind joining me and Robin in my office. I think it's time for your performance review," he said, smiling all the while.

9

HOUSTON, WE'VE GOT SOME PROBLEMS

Suffice to say, the ride back to the mall for Brandon was even more troublesome than the ride from it. Somehow the shit show outside was only deepening in depth and stench. As Brandon frantically drove, he witnessed scores of insanities such as brawls, impromptu parties, shameless looting, and even a block-wide orgy. Yes, an orgy. Brandon had to slow down for that one as it had bled out into the street in a brilliant display of tantric yoga, body part worship and awkward BDSM. Even the roads less traveled were proving difficult as he was forced to shake a deranged looter with a hard-on from his vehicle's hood. Finally and gratefully, Brandon reached his destination, running inside for advice and counsel.

Still wrapping his brain around the insanity he was forced to process, Brandon made his way through the mall in search of Cliff. The sage-like custodian had always been adept at offering wisdom in such situations. Sifting through the crowded center, Brandon at last spotted Cliff in front of the electronics store. Focusing on his friend, Brandon sifted through the crowd to reach his destination.

Reaching Cliff, Brandon was surprised to see him fixated on the television. Programs were interrupted with breaking news worldwide. Apparently what Brandon had witnessed in his journey to and from home was no isolated incident. Cliff watched the TV rigidly along with his fellow custodians Ron, Michael, and Dennis.

Without looking over, Cliff acknowledged his presence. "Well hello again, Brandon. I thought you went home for the day," said Cliff.

Brandon nodded. "Yeah, I tried. Things there are…strange to say the least. I was hoping to talk to you about it," he said.

Ron shook his head. "Brandon, ya'll need a system. I keep telling you to have that couple you live with to put a sock on the door or something so you don't walk in on anymore of their kinky shit," he offered.

Brandon shook his head. "Believe me, this is one of those times I wish it had been the kinky shit," he replied.

Michael Metz looked over at Brandon. The stoic custodian was the biggest of the four. Mike kept his dark beard and hair short and well-kept and possessed a reserved warmth and humor. And while he was the quietest of the bunch, he could speak volumes with a look. Mike had a reputation of being an honest friend, reliable coworker, and a hilarious drunk. "What's up, and do we really want to know?"

"Josh and Sarah are kinky as fuck. Of course we want to know," added Dennis Butel. The only one of the bunch without facial hair, Dennis was known for his big heart and friendly immersion in pervery.

“Those two sure do get busier than a cat covering crap on a marble floor,” added Ron.

Cliff held up a hand to silence his crew. “What’s going on, Brandon?”

Brandon looked about before leaning in so that only the crew could hear what he had to say. “Well, let’s just say the both of them had a reaction to the Omega vaccine,” he offered.

Cliff raised an eyebrow. “Like an allergic one?”

“More like they are fucking vampires now,” said Brandon.

“No shit?” said Dennis.

“Well if that don’t make a preacher cuss, nothing will,” said Ron.

“Could you elaborate?” asked Michael.

“I mean that’s some crazy ass shit,” replied Ron.

“I meant Brandon,” said Michael

Brandon nodded. “Sure. They are pale, super strong, hard as stone and have fangs. I didn’t stick around long enough to test the blood part,” he replied.

Cliff absorbed this, nodding. “You probably did the right thing. But if they are vampires or even close to it, they are going to need blood. I suggest you pick up some raw fare for them, maybe even a pet shop visit. That way your neighbors don’t get turned into a meal accidently on purpose,” he said.

Brandon shuddered at the thought of picking up anything for bloodletting but worked through it. “You don’t think that is crazy at all or a little weird?” he asked.

Cliff jerked a thumb at the TV. “Brandon, the whole world’s a shit show right now. I would just make sure you had all avenues covered is all. And it wouldn’t hurt to stock up while you are there. This is definitely going to get worse before it ever gets better,” he said.

Brandon nodded. "Yeah, you're likely right. You wouldn't by chance have seen my brother around have you?"

Michael pointed to the door. "I saw him leave not long ago. Looked like he walked out on his job happily," he said.

"Oh great," said Brandon.

Ron shook his head. "I don't know how that worked out, Brandon. You're a good kid. That brother of yours has only got one oar in the water if you catch my drift."

"Believe me, I do, and I get that a lot," said Brandon as he shook Cliff's hand. "Thanks, Cliff. I better get on that. Hopefully I'll find Aaron at home too. I'll see you guys around," he said.

"See ya, B," said Ron.

"Take care, man," said Michael as Dennis gave a little salute.

"Brandon, you be careful out there," said Cliff.

"I will," said Brandon with a nod before he was off.

The four custodians resumed their vigil upon the TV screen as the events they witnessed grew crazier by the minute. None of the four men could remove their eyes from the news as it all somehow felt like a dream. Yet the unrest rising within the mall reminded them all that what they saw was very much real. It was hard to find the words to convey such a moment.

Unless of course, you happen to be Ron.

"Well, butter my ass and call me a biscuit, feels like the world's been ate by a wolf and shit over a cliff. And I mean a ledge, not you, Cliff," said Ron.

"Kinky," said Dennis.

"God damnit, Ron," said Cliff.

Rushing back out to his car, Brandon made his way to the nearest grocery store. He wasn't the only one stocking up on food, so the going was slow. He acquired what he could afford before rushing out again. Brandon then made a quick run to the nearest pet store. There was, by far, much less traffic there. Without explaining why to the cashier, Brandon purchased 20 of their rats, as it was the only thing he could stomach sacrificing.

With everything acquired, Brandon made a beeline home, trying to maintain tunnel vision and devoid of distraction. Surprisingly he was already tired of seeing freeloading looters running about proudly with their wangs loose. Pulling in again to his parking lot, Brandon couldn't remember a time he was more relieved to be home. Grabbing the bag of groceries, he headed for his door, ready to face the challenge of his roommates.

Little did Brandon know, however, was that there was some shit just waiting for him before it hit the fan.

Brandon suddenly heard a raw, primal scream as his head shot up toward his apartment. At that precise moment, the door to his home exploded open as his roommate Josh came flying out of their pad. Brandon dropped the groceries as he dove out of the way. Josh crashed upon the hood of the neighbor's car before quickly recovering. Wearing only pants and chiseled features, Brandon's transformed friend looked ready to open a few cans of fresh whoop ass.

"Alright, that's it, you flaky fuck. It's on!" he challenged before rushing back inside in a furious blur.

Shaking his head clear, Brandon clamored to his feet and rushed into his place. Entering, he gasped at the utter shitstorm that had become of his home. Every bit of furniture was destroyed. The walls had several holes from what appeared to be relentless combat and furious sex. His neighbor Jordan was laid out in a Rubbermaid hamper, legs and arms trellised like a stuffed turkey. Jordan was sporting only boxers and several bites across his body while appearing basted in grease. Gagged as he was, he looked at Brandon with pleading eyes, wanting either released from his misery or killed outright.

And then Brandon saw his roomies. Sarah was yelling for Josh and Aaron to calm down as the two engaged in an escalating bout of fisticuffs. Joshua appeared ready to kill Brandon's brother, while Aaron looked chill as fuck as he beckoned Josh to bring it on. The foundation of the apartment looked like it could withstand little if any more.

"You've fucked with my last nerve for the last fucking time," said Josh with a growl. "You are either leaving here in a body bag or with my foot in your ass. But one way or the other, you are leaving."

"I don't sweat you anymore, asshole. Let's see what you got," challenged Aaron as he hopped up and down like a prize fighter ready for the bell to ring.

"Oh, we are doing this shit," said Josh as he charged at Aaron.

Brandon watched as his brother exerted his will and Josh appeared to run into an invisible wall. Josh suddenly was pushed backward, and he fought against it with his considerable strength. Using his enhanced speed, Josh shot to the left in a blur and the force that was pressing on him slammed against the wall. Brandon shielded himself as he watched in horror at the destruction of the place he once called home.

Josh surged again, getting himself and his outstretched hand within an inch for Aaron. Brandon's brother strained, apparently using his mind to keep Joshua from choking the ever-loving shit out of him. Joshua grinned as he slowly plodded forward and Aaron gathered himself to try and push his roommate back.

Finally, Brandon could stand it no longer. "ALL RIGHT, WHAT IN THE ACTUAL NAME OF ALL GIVEN FUCKS IS GOING ON IN HERE?!"

Josh and Aaron stopped their fighting immediately, looking like abashed, busted children. Sarah lowered her head, shaking it morosely as Brandon looked at all of them in turn. Josh tried to justify the fight, tried to word it in a way that Brandon would understand his reasoning for wanting to rip his friend's brother in half.

"Bro, he started it, man. That I can assure you," said Josh. In hindsight for Josh, that was certainly not the right defense.

Brandon's eyes practically set ablaze as he held up one hand, indicating ever so plainly for his friends that it was time to shut the fuck up. "Nope. Nope. No, sir. Don't want to hear it. Not even a little bit. Look at this fucking place! There is no logical excuse to tear our home into the shreds that we now stand within. Not a one!"

Aaron pointed at Joshua and Sarah. "You didn't tell me these fuckers were bloodsucking vampires now."

Sarah chimed in. "And you didn't tell us he was straight out of a comic book with superpowers now."

Brandon waved his hands for silence. "Oh no. No, no! This is not Brandon's fault. I have been all over either looking for or getting shit for you three and I come the fuck home and this is what is waiting for me," he said, still trying to grasp the carnage wrought as he internally bid farewell to his security deposit. Finally, his eyes set on Jordan as he pointed to their neighbor who was clearly in duress. "And what the hell is this shit? Why is our neighbor done up like a fucking holiday turkey? Did Thanksgiving come early? Did we become cannibals? Cause I certainly didn't get that fucking memo."

Josh grimaced. "Yeah, about that, bro. Shit just kinda escalated. I mean Jordan's a dick. And we were hungry, and it went from there. We started trying bites and seeing what went good with the blood and all and before you know it, it started looking like the holidays."

"I see," said Brandon as he evaluated Joshua calmly. "And did it ever occur to you that what you were doing was wrong and, oh, I don't know, against the law and could bring some serious fucking trouble on us all?"

Sarah nodded. "Of course it did, Brandon.

"Yeah, bro," said Joshua, pointing at Jordan. "That's why we didn't kill the asshole."

Brandon threw his hands in the air, looking to the sky as if wondering why the gods had sentenced him to such a metaphorical dicking. "Oh, well there we go. That makes it so much fucking better. Thanks for only giving him physical and mental trauma and not killing him. That will give us so much lenience from the judge at the hearing!"

"That was kind of our thought too," said Josh, apologetically. "Sorry, man."

Brandon ran his hands over his face. "For which part, Josh? Cause the way I see it, sorry is just the cover fee for the shit storm of apologies needed for this." Brandon then looked about the apartment and then to his brother. "And what about you? What's your story?"

Aaron shrugged. "Like them, I guess," he said before pointing to his arm. "Vaccine."

"I see," said Brandon. "And instead of turning you into an instinct-driven, vampric nightmare, it gave you powers?"

Aaron nodded. "Yup. And I'm pretty fucking stoked about it," he replied.

"I bet," said Brandon. "No way you won't go to the Dark Side with that shit if you haven't already."

"The less you know the better then," offered Aaron.

"I'm sure," said Brandon as he looked between the three of them. "So, this is how it is going to go down. I am separating you three. Aaron is coming with me. We are getting supplies and preparing to weather this major shitstorm that's showing no signs of letting up. If you all got weird ass attributes from the vaccine, you can damn well be sure you aren't the only ones. There's no way this isn't getting worse before it gets better."

"But I just got here," said Aaron.

Brandon's eyes flared as he offered his brother a violent gaze. "Shut. The. Fuck. Up," he stated adamantly. "That was not a request in the fucking slightest. And as for you two," he said, pointing to the vampire couple.

"You want us to get dinner ready?" asked Sarah expectantly.

Brandon continued like he didn't hear her. "You all start cleaning this place up. And for the fuckest of sakes, let Jordan go. And whatever you do, don't leave home. We will be back when we can and together we will figure all this shit out. Until then, be on your best and merriest behaviors and don't drive me to drinking or welcoming suicide with open arms. Are we clear?"

Josh scratched the back of his neck in thought. "You sure you want us to let Jordan go? I mean sure he's in a compromising situation, but he's still also a dick. If we keep him alive but contained, it balances out somehow."

Brandon stared angrily at Josh before going to where Jordan was still prepped and basted. Kneeling, he spoke to his neighbor. "So, Jordan. I understand that this has been a hard day for you and that my roomies are a handful. But I am going to have to have your word now. If we let you go, are you going to promise to leave this between us? I mean, I would hate to see what happened if you called the police on two vampires and an apparent telekinetic. I'm fairly sure my brother could crush your nuts with his mind before Josh and Sarah drain you dry."

"He's right. I could," added Aaron.

"And you don't taste too bad with a garlic infusion," said Joshua.

Brandon nodded. "So, what do you say, Jordan? Are we cool? Or are we at least cool enough that we can be live and let live?" Jordan nodded passionately with tears in his eyes. Brandon patted his head before standing again. "Good. I'm not going to remove the tape because if I hear you talk I may change my mind. It has been that kind of day. Let's go, Aaron."

"Do I gotta?" whined Aaron.

"Fucking A right you do," replied Brandon. "I'm going to need you. Our friends are going to need us. And when shit goes real south, I am sure you are going to want to get Shawna the fuck out of Dodge."

Aaron lowered his head and sighed. "Fuck. Fine, I'll go," he said before following Brandon out. "But if she brings up anything about her boyfriend, you don't know nothing."

"And if you don't tell me what the hell you did, I won't," replied Brandon.

"Cool," said Aaron.

"Hey, B," said Josh as his friend turned to look at him. "You be careful out there, man."

Brandon gave him a nod. "See you when we get back," he offered, and then he was gone.

Joshua and Sarah looked about the ransacked apartment, where little, if any furniture had survived the havoc. "Wow, we've gone and made a fuckery of this, haven't we, babe?"

"Yeah, we did," whispered Sarah.

"I guess we should get started," said Josh.

"No time like now," offered Sarah.

"Of course," started Josh, "it probably wouldn't hurt to have a little bite first."

Sarah grinned. "Yeah, I think Jordan has a little more he could spare," she replied.

"You get the baster and the condiments, and I'll get him ready," said Josh as the two lovers hopped to it.

And there, in his makeshift platter, Jordan saw his life flash before his eyes as he wondered if things could get any worse.

Of course, he would soon find out that they could.

And they did.

10

THINGS GET WEIRD, LIKE REALLY WEIRD

Driving swiftly in his Prius, or at least as swiftly as a Prius can take you, Brandon made a hasty return to the mall yet again. He felt a swelling pit of uneasiness sitting in his gut, somehow knowing that they were on the brink of a worldwide, category-five shitstorm. Every trip to and from the mall was shittier than the last. Fires now erupted sporadically as mischief and mayhem increased. Brandon now felt like the meat inside a clusterfuck sandwich served up with a side of steaming bullshit.

Life is just funny like that.

As Brandon evaded wrecks, fleeing civilians, and abandoned vehicles, he noticed that navigating the roads was one step closer to impossible. On one stretch they were chased by a group of bloodied men and women driven to fury. The name calling his ears picked up was quite appalling.

A time or two Brandon had to traverse the sidewalks to get where he needed to go.

"This is why you don't get the Prius," said Aaron from the passenger seat. "It's just not made for this kind of shit."

Brandon gritted his teeth and shook his head. "This from the carless squatter who hasn't driven since high school. One of us has to be responsible here, and you abdicated any claims to that title at childbirth. I had to get the fucking Prius, grateful that I was able to get a color other than powder-fucking blue. It's a responsible car with great mileage. Perfect for when you have to run errands or take your brother every god damn place in the city cause he can't be bothered with things like having his own reliable transportation."

Aaron responded as he kept his eyes intently upon the road. "I see it's a sore subject. I'll leave it alone for the time being."

Brandon took another corner sharply as he responded. "As you are coming to realize, just about everything is a sore fucking subject right now. The world's gone ass first on a hot poker forged in hell and I am still having to lecture my god damn brother on the need to be more mature! This is not how I ever planned on spending the end of times."

"So, you have given this some thought?" asked Aaron.

"Not extensively, no," said Brandon dodging an orange cone. "But you catch right book or movie and you start asking yourself those 'what if' questions."

"We gotta get you another hobby. Or laid," mused Aaron.

Brandon growled. "Well I am sorry, I guess you've never had the luxury of bringing a date home to find your brother buck-ass nude in your bed with his butt cheeks in the air and cuddling with a Playstation controller before. It does kinda sorta ruin the whole motherfucking mood!"

“You know I can’t help the fact I have a nice ass,” said Aaron.

“Fuck you and the ass that carried you in,” spat Brandon angrily. “Now hold on!”

Gunning his Prius, Brandon traversed a harrowing route through peril. People ambled on the street into oncoming traffic, pointing and grunting as they did. Cars swerved to avoid them, causing multiple accidents. Aaron did his best to assist in his own way, flipping off those who endangered their travel while telling them what they could sit and spin on. Making it to a relatively clear stretch of road, Brandon finally allowed himself to breathe as he tried to slow his heartrate back down.

Aaron finally let his lingering thought emerged. "And tell me, why are we going back to the mall again?"

Brandon kept his eyes on the road as he replied. "We need supplies. We need to let our friends know what’s going on. And you need to be there for Shawna."

Aaron snorted at this, shaking his head. "Shawna would rather smoke a festering turd laced with SPAM and maggots in the part of hell where they play nothing but Justin Beiber and show Barney reruns that talk to me."

"That’s a pretty sick level of hell," observed Brandon as he maintained his intensity. "But it still doesn't change the fact that you love her. Don't think I don't know why you have been such a giver of no fucks these past few months. It's the only reason I haven't thrown your ass out of the apartment yet."

Aaron shook his head, holding now to the "oh shit handle." "You don't know what the hell you’re talking about," he mumbled.

"I think I do," said Brandon firmly. "You were always a shit and you will always be a shit. But you were by far less of a shit when you were with her. Shawna brought out a lot of good in you and without her you just want to wallow in more shit. And you have let things get pretty damn shitty lately."

"No putting anything passed you is there?" said Aaron.

"I've my faults but being unobservant is not one of them."

Both brothers then saw the jam forming up ahead. A big wreck involving a semi and an ambulance blocked their way. More stiff-looking citizens ambled around the wreckage as cars began to clog the intersection. It was evident that getting around the congestion was going to be an impossibility.

"Well this puts a damper on things," said Brandon.

"I guess we gotta go back home," said Aaron.

"Oh, I think the fuck not," said Brandon as he slapped his brother on the chest. "Aren't you supposed to have some fucking superpowers now?"

Aaron smiled in recognition. "Oh yeah," he said.

"Well then, do something with them already!"

"Fine," grumbled Aaron as he rolled down his window and stuck his arms and torso out of the Prius.

Holding out his right hand while bracing himself with the left, Aaron began to focus intensely. Had Brandon been able to see his face he would have noted he looked equal parts confused and constipated. Yet Aaron persisted, imagining his next moves as he let his intensity make out with his imagination.

To Brandon's surprise, he watched as the congestion before them parted like the Red Sea. People, clutter, and broken vehicles were pushed aside, revealing an open road. Brandon wasted none of the moment and floored it again. He and his brother sailed through the parting with Aaron laughing and pointing to himself, indicating "yeah, that was fucking me" to those that watched on in astonishment.

"Great," said Brandon distractedly. "The Force is strong with this one. We're all rightly fucked."

But Aaron could not hear Brandon then. He was once more engaged in his newfound powers which made even the best video games paltry in comparison. Aaron moved his hands about as if conducting a symphony, batting his attention here and there. He even began to hum a pleasant tune as he synchronized it with his tomfoolery.

As Brandon pressed toward their destination, Aaron continued to orchestrate his sonata of shenanigans. He kept the route before the Prius clear, yet he chose to do so in the most dickish of manners. Some people he lifted telekinetically by their underwear, others he offered a power-infused push that knocked them on their asses. Aaron caused hydrants to burst, pulled a six-pack of beer to himself and did severe cosmetic damage to a closed Subway, indicating his strong dislike for the chain.

Pulling a beer from the bunch, he cracked it open as he offered the cluster to Brandon. "Hot damn, this is fun! You want a brew?"

Brandon reached over, grabbing his brother by the back of his jeans and yanking him back into the vehicle. "Get your ass back in here!"

Aaron wiped spilled beer from his shirt. "Make up your fucking mind already!"

"I said clear us a path, not further your own journey toward the Dark Side!"

Aaron shrugged. "What's the use of superpowers if you can't exploit the shit out of them every now and then?" he asked before chugging the beer and tossing the can out the window. Before it hit the ground, Aaron willed it to pelt a driver honking and yelling at them from his vehicle.

"If society collapsing doesn't kill us, you surely will," observed Brandon grimly.

Aaron's eyes lit up like a pinball machine as he grinned at Brandon. "Dude! I bet I can fucking make this car fly. We could be flying right now! What do you think?"

"Don't even fucking think it!" roared Brandon as he made another sharp turn.

"Buzzkill," crooned Aaron as he slumped in his seat and opened another beer.

The remainder of their journey was uneventful save for Aaron's inventive assaults with empty beer cans. Brandon at last reached the mall and pulled into the parking lot yet again. People were rushing into the mall as others did their best to vacate the premises in a disorderly fashion. Brandon and Aaron exchanged a glance before exiting the car and heading inside. Their way was pretty much clear as Aaron used a telekinetic bubble around them to ensure their "personal space."

Brandon ventured into the mall, alert and at the ready as his brother strutted merrily next to him. It was obvious Aaron didn't have a care in the world, which made him far more dangerous now that he was enhanced as he was. Trying to perish such thoughts, Brandon looked about for the wise custodian Cliff as well as Shawna as they waded through the growing unease that was the populace.

As Brandon made his way through the food court, he was forced to evade fleeing patrons. The flood court was cluttered with trash and discarded food as people made hasty exits or took a chance at free food. There was still obviously some confusion in the majority as to whether they should be entering the mall or fleeing it. Aaron, sincerely gave no fucks regardless, grateful that he had brought the remaining beer with him.

Looking through the ever-flowing crowd, Brandon finally grinned as he saw Cliff and his group. "Thank god," he said as he pointed. "There they are."

Approaching the brothers was Cliff, Ron, Michael, Dennis, and David. Brandon was relieved to see them all and Aaron was damn happy to see his coworker as they all approached one another. All the custodians held to mops and brooms and appeared prepared for all sorts of hells to break loose. The grimness on Cliff's face was all Brandon needed to access the current situation.

"Cliff!" hollered Brandon as he finally reached the head custodian. "I see things aren't much better in here than they are outside."

"They're only getting worse," said Cliff as he looked about warily. "And I fear this is only the beginning."

Aaron threw an arm around David, offering him one of his last two beers. "Well it's always good to have a friend during a shit storm," he said before the two clinked their cans and drained the beers.

"Just like you to only bring me one cervesa, pinche gringo," said David unapprovingly.

Brandon continued with Cliff. "I'm thinking this vaccine was not as good as people hoped. I've seen a shit ton of symptoms that would say otherwise."

"You mean like your roomies becoming fang-bearing Count Suckulas," offered Ron.

"That is one of them, yes," replied Brandon. "But it is doing more than that. I have seen all kinds of crap to and from the mall today. And this fucker here has superpowers now," he added, pushing his brother's arm.

"Guilty as charged," crowed Aaron.

"No shit?" David asked.

"No shit, David," replied Aaron.

"Da-veed. No need to be a super asshole," said David.

"Some fuckers have all the luck," said Dennis, scowling at Aaron.

"I know right?" said Aaron unapologetically. "Luck finally shined on a dog's ass."

"What the hell do we do now, Cliff?" Brandon asked, ignoring his brother.

Cliff shook his head. "I haven't the foggiest notion. This level of madness is beyond my ability to process fully."

Just then, the group jumped at the sound of gunfire. Looking about, the screaming in the mall increased as many who were trying to exit the mall were now returning in droves. Brandon and the others looked toward the doors as the intensity of the gun blasts increased. Cliff and his comrades held their mops and brooms at the ready as Aaron released the carbonated buildup within him with a sudsy burp.

Soon, a group of ten men entered the mall sporting some serious macho-dick, hick-like swagger. The entire group was armed to the teeth with various firearms and looked like Walking Dead wannabes. It was apparent they were flush with victorious glee as they whooped and hollered and dealt out high fives to one another. Brandon and his friends watched them suspiciously as they bordered on being penalized for excessive celebration.

Slinging his assault rifle over his shoulder, the loudest of the bunch held out his hands for quiet. The man was a cluster of muscle and beer belly, wearing tight jeans, black combat boots, a patriotic t-shirt and an eagle crested bandana on his head. His thick face was clean-shaven, and Brandon watched as the man paused to take a selfie with his crew before he resumed his attention on the mall patrons. "All right, people, settle on down now. We've got the situation well under control. You just sit tight in here and let us handle the problem now," said the man.

Without hesitance, Cliff marched over to the man and his group. His own rag-tag band followed quickly behind, obviously unimpressed with the display of weapon-heavy bravado being utilized. Brandon soon accompanied them with Aaron and David reluctantly following along. "What in the hell do you think you are doing?" demanded Cliff as he neared the group.

The gun-toting leader smiled easily at Cliff, revealing severely bleached white teeth. "Just our part in saving your lives, friends. In case you didn't notice, there's a war going on out there and we're here to strike back. So, you're welcome," he said.

"And you all are?" asked Cliff.

The man grinned proudly. "We're the Justice Enforcers. The name's Randal and this is my crew. We've been preparing for this day for a while now, so rest assured when I tell you that you're in good hands."

Cliff exchanged glances with Ron. "Thoughts?"

Ron shook his head. "I don't know about you, Cliff, but I got a feeling this guy can dig both hands in his back pockets and still not find his ass. I certainly don't feel any safer."

"Agreed," said Cliff, before speaking to Randal again. "So, Randal, what exactly are you shooting out there?"

"Zombies," replied Randal as he pointed toward the doors. "There's a whole mess of the fuckers out there. We fought our way to the mall, taking out every one of them we could."

Brandon looked at Randal curiously. "And were these 'zombies' actually causing any harm?"

A thin, pale man in camouflage next to Randal spoke after pumping his shotgun. "We didn't give them a chance. One good shot and they went down like sacks of bricks."

Cliff grunted. "Sounds like you guys were just itching for an excuse to use all those guns," he observed, pointing to the group.

"We know what we're doing," said Randal. "We've prepared for this kind of thing for years now."

"How?" asked Brandon. "Watching TV shows? Playing video games?"

"We also did drills and stuff," said another guy adorned with a Rambo-like bandana.

"Like paintball? LARPing?" inquired Brandon.

The man with the bandana lowered his head "Yeah," he mumbled.

Brandon looked at Cliff. "I have a horrible feeling about this for some reason," he offered.

"You and I both," said Cliff as he approached Randal. "I don't know why you felt like you had the right to go on a shooting spree, but you are not welcome here. I suggest you take your merry band of gun enthusiasts and call it a day."

Randal shook his head. "I think you misunderstood. We're here now and we're here to stay. The people in this mall are going to need protecting and that's what we are going to do," he said.

"And who is going to protect them from you?" demanded Michael.

"No need for that," said Randal. "We have this all under control.

"I'm willing to wager you don't even have premature ejaculation under control," countered Ron as he jerked a thumb toward one of Randal's men. "Look at that little fucker on the end there, he's hard and horny to shoot some more." The guy at the end blushed, for Ron was right on both accounts.

"I'm afraid my associate is right," said Cliff. "Please leave before we have to remove you."

Randal shook his head. "That ain't gonna happen. We came prepared with guns, and what do you got between you? A couple of brooms and mops?"

"And more sense than ya'll can shake a stick at," said Ron.

"Not good odds," replied Randal.

Brandon stepped between Cliff and Randal, placing a hand on the chests of both. "Come on, guys. There's no need to fight. I think there's enough crazy to go around for all of us already," he said.

Randal removed Brandon's hand from his chest. "If we aren't listening to your friend, we sure as hell ain't listening to you either," stated Randal.

"That's unfortunate," said Brandon as he nodded to his brother. "Cause you see, we are not without our own wiles."

"What the hell is that supposed to mean?" asked Randal before his eyes went wide. "What the shit?"

Much to Randal's surprise, his right arm raised without his control and buried itself in his groin. Randal cried out and gasped for breath as he dropped to his knees. His eyes watered as he briefly wished for death. Randal's comrades jumped away from Randal before they trained their guns on Brandon and his friends.

It was then that the shotgun the man in camouflage held jumped from his hands. As the thin fellow watched it with wildly, the shotgun spun once swiftly, and smacked the man in the face. As he fell, the shotgun landed in Cliff's hands who trained it on the others. As a standoff began, the remaining members of Randal's group all fought against Aaron as he made them all jimmy-punch themselves harshly.

As his custodians armed themselves with some of Randal's men's firepower, Cliff grinned at Randal. "Well I do believe the tables have turned, good sir. And so, I will restate my initial demand that you and your lackeys vacate my mall with haste."

"What the fuck was all that," choked Randal through his pain.

"Real justice, bitches," said Aaron proudly, still admiring his handiwork.

"We will give you a few seconds to catch your breaths, then I suggest you be on your merry way, minus the guns," said Cliff.

"We ain't going anywhere without our gear," spat Randal. He then gasped as his hand raised again despite his will. "Alright, alright! Just don't do that no more," he whimpered.

"Well he does have a lick of sense," said Ron. "Surprise, surprise."

Just then, everyone involved was distracted by slamming upon the doors. Turning, their horror and surprise intensified as they came face to face with what appeared to be real zombies. Bloodied and marred by gunshot wounds, the zombies had gathered and swarmed, looking hungrily upon Randal's group with lifeless, yet furious eyes. The swarm began banging on the doors and the glass began to quickly crack.

"Well holy hills of Christ," said Brandon in hushed tones. "Looks like you and yours really called down the fucking thunder."

The thin fellow in the camouflage pointed to one of the angry dead. "But I killed you," he whined.

"I think you just pissed him off, friend," said Ron.

Cliff looked angrily at Randal. "How many people did you shoot?"

“I wouldn’t say too many. Just the deserving,” said Randal.

“How many?!” roared Cliff.

“Maybe a hundred or so,” said Randal.

“Holy fucking shit,” said Cliff.

Just then, the doors gave way and broke as the pissed off undead hoard swarmed toward Randal and his band of enforcers. With an insatiable hunger for blood and vengeance, they rushed angrily and swiftly, ready to feed and devour those responsible for the pain inflicted on them.

Randal’s men could not recover quickly enough or break the fear being unarmed cast upon them. The undead swarmed them and in seconds blood spewed in great founts as all the proud group of wannabes screamed their last breaths. Randal barely avoided the initial assault as the feeding on his friends halted the zombie advance at least momentarily. Cliff and his crew watched in horror knowing they were powerless to help as karma wrought its just desserts.

At the sight of blood spilling and spraying about, Brandon practically fainted. Cliff lunged over, catching the man and throwing him over his shoulder. He then motioned to the others before backing away. "Fall back, men. Don't draw attention to us unless you have to," he commanded.

"No need to tell us twice," said Ron as he and the others kept their newly acquired weapons at the ready.

"You heard the man," said Michael as he grabbed Randal and dragged him along. He was of course, the only one present that could budge someone like Randal. "Let's move."

"I don't understand," said Randal, practically in tears. "What is happening?"

"You done fucked up, that's what's happening," said Cliff as he then talked over his shoulder. "How are you holding up back there, Brandon?"

"Oh, I'm fine now. Just a little shaky. Thanks for the save," he offered dreamily.

As more zombies swelled at the doors, the food present was no longer enough. One of them pointed at Randal and the others. "Food. Feed!" it rasped bitterly, it's eyes ablaze with hunger.

"Try the pizza," said Aaron as he slowly backed away. He then pointed to Randal. "Or this asshole."

The bullet ridden zombie set its sights on Randal. "Feed. Asshole," he uttered.

"What the fuck, man?" said Randal.

"You made this bed, now get eaten in it," said Aaron.

"Keep moving!" ordered Cliff as he began to retreat. "Brandon, cover my ass," he instructed before handing back the shotgun.

“Well even from a heterosexual standpoint, I can say it’s a nice ass, Cliff. Custodial work has been good to it I think,” said Brandon.

“I mean cover our six, bud.”

Brandon took the weapon hazily. "Oh, sure," he said, still loopy. "Lemme bust the caps that makes the zombies fall down."

The group hastened their retreat. In their departure, the last screams from Randal’s men died out at last. What remained then was the sound of tearing flesh as the food court became an all-you-can-eat buffet with no holds barred. When most of Randal's men devoured, the zombies shifted their attention to other endeavors, which frankly was anyone else that was alive. Cliff lead the retreat while the other custodians covered their withdrawal. Brandon fired the shotgun semi successfully, giggling as he did and managing moderate success.

Keeping close to the group, David turned to Aaron. "You know, man. You got powers and shit now, gringo. Use them."

"I keep forgetting," said Aaron, which was mostly a lie.

Seeing a zombie rushing them and getting too close for comfort, Aaron reached out with his powers, seizing the zombie completely. Confused, the zombie grunted and struggled but was powerless against Aaron's abilities. Aaron then turned the zombie around to face his fellow zombies. With the zombie's limbs under his full control, Aaron acted as an insane puppeteer, forcing his zombie to enact moves straight out of a Kung-Fu flick, adding the occasional "Hi-yah" or "Wa-tah" for emphasis.

The group almost had to give pause at the spectacle. A confused zombie grunted and whined as he involuntarily beat the shit out of his comrades. Undead fists of fury spread across the end of the food court, dropping hungry fiends like bad habits. When it was all said and done, Aaron had, through his own love of mischief, afforded the group some much needed breathing room to make their escape. For his finale, he lifted the zombie with his mind, spun him like a propeller and hurled him into the thickest patch of remaining zombies.

"Crude, twisted, but effective," murmured Dennis.

Aaron beamed at his handiwork. "Why Magneto never did that with Wolverine to take care of the rest of the X-Men is beyond me."

"What did I miss? And why is my ass numb?" said Brandon.

"Hang tight, buddy, we're almost there," offered Cliff as he ran on. Cliff lead the group quickly to the Dabbles and Dorkery store. Seeing Jim defending his place of business with a ball bat, Cliff waved to get his attention. "Get ready to close the doors. We'll cover you!"

"On it," said Jim as he ran inside.

Reaching the store, Cliff and his crew set up a wall in front as Jim ran behind the counter to activate closing procedures. Soon a rumbling was heard as the security grille lowered from above to secure the store. Halfway down, Cliff and the others ventured inside, waiting for the grille to secure them from the rest of the mall. Cliff set Brandon down as everyone breathed a major sigh of relief.

And then that one dick of a zombie came sliding under the grille to keep the shit rolling.

The zombie, a bald, enraged, brute of a man who had been shot in the neck surged the line of custodians. Pushing Dennis and Michael out of the way, the zombie grabbed hold of Randal. Randal was unable to hold the zombie back as it sunk its teeth into his shoulder. Randal screamed out for help as the others rushed to his aid.

Grabbing the top of the zombie's head and lodging his fingers into the eyes, Ron was able to pull the zombie away as Cliff and Brandon grabbed Randal. Or at least Cliff did. Brandon tried but when blood spattered on him it sent him to the ground faster than all get out. Ron pulled the creature away, grabbing it by the shirt as well before yanking hard.

"Alright you fast eatin' sumbitch, I've had a enough of this already!" said Ron pulled the zombie to face him, kicked it in the gonads before twisting around, wrapping his arms around its head, and hopping to land on his ass as he brought the zombie with him.

The motion and the pull Ron placed on the zombie as he landed coupled with the neck injury the zombie held was enough for Ron to be able to tear the creature's head clean off. The zombie's body stumbled backwards, floundering about blindly before it smashed into the security grill and flopped upon the ground still spasming. Ron looked at the head in his hands, felt the blood down his back as he tossed the decapitated head aside and grimaced. Standing, he rubbed at his hind end as he shook his head.

"Always wanted to do that in real life, but the landing felt like a prostate exam gone way wrong," said Ron as he looked at his bloody shoulder. "Great. Fucker slimed me too," he added.

Everyone then focused on Randal, who was screaming in agony and clutching his shoulder as blood oozed out of his bite wound. Cliff tried to calm him yet was unsuccessful. He couldn't even get Randal to let him clean and dress the wound. Aaron covered his ears as everyone else looked at one another trying to decide what to do.

"We need to get him calm and address that bite," said Cliff as he continued to work with Randal.

Michael knelt on the opposite side of Randal from Cliff as he tried to help. “I know a few relaxation techniques," he offered as he placed a hand under Randal's back. "Not to worry, man. I will have you pain free in no time."

Running a hand over Randal's head and cheek, Michael then lifted his chin slightly upward as Randal looked at him desperately. Satisfied at the positioning, Michael surprised Randal with a mighty left hook across his raised chin that rocked the man's head and sent him sprawling further on the ground. Slumping and silencing almost immediately, a tranquil quiet settled over the store as Michael nodded approvingly.

"That ought to give us plenty of time to patch him up," said Michael.

"Didn't know you were going to use an all-natural cranial anesthesia," said Brandon, observing but keeping his field of vision away from the wound. He looked at his boss then. "Jim, could you fetch the first aid kit?"

With the kit fetched and Michael and Cliff working on Randal, Aaron watched the man disapprovingly. "Look, I'm not trying to be a bigger dick than usual, but I have seen enough movies to know that him getting bit ain't a good thing."

"We will cross that road when we get there," said Cliff without looking up from his work. "We don't know what is true or not with the effects of the vaccine, other than it affects people in different ways. Until we know we will do our best to get through this and make the hard decisions when we have to."

"We shouldn't wait too long. In my defense he's kind of a horse's ass as is and I'd hate to see him turned to something worse," replied Aaron.

"Regardless," said Cliff more sternly. "I think there are enough people dying in the mall right now, we don't need to add to it ourselves."

"Have it your way," said Aaron, shrugging as he wished for another beer. "But if he starts turning, I'm gonna telekinetically twist him in a way he would have to eat his own ass."

"You are into the kinky shit too aren't you, man? I can respect that," said Dennis as he tried to look through the security grille at events unfolding. "What's our next step, Cliff?"

Cliff shook his head as he finished administering a bandage to the cleaned bite wound. "Let's catch our breath. Once we do that, we are going to have to get back out there. We can't stay in here forever and there are people dying. I don't know about you, but I don't want that on my conscience."

"My conscience is cool," offered Aaron nonchalantly. "This wasn't our fault that this happened and we sure as hell didn't assist Randal and his buddies in making it worse. I say we get out while the getting is still good."

"That's not our way," said Michael, looking at Aaron severely.

Aaron shrugged. "But it's mine. I am not in to fighting fights that aren't mine," he replied as he looked at the owner of the store. "With all due respect, I am going to take the back way out of here, see if I can find myself a bowl, light that shit up and sit this one out till the world's done burning."

At this, Brandon stood and approached his brother. By his anger and courage in that moment, you would never have been able to tell that it wasn't him that had the superpowers. "That's horseshit and you know it," he offered, inching even closer to Aaron's face.

Aaron held out his hands apologetically. "It is what it is, brother of mine. I just want us the hell out of this death trap. I'm no superhero," he said before pointing to the custodians. "And they are no saviors," he added before pointing to David. "And the one and only way this guy will be of use is if fucking these creatures would cure them."

"I would be good at this, yes," mused David, nodding to himself, lost in visualization.

Brandon clenched his fists as he battled his own anger and impatience. "It doesn't matter what we are. It doesn't matter what you think we are. The bottom line is there are those that need us. We all have those we care about out there, and I'll be damned if I am going to let you sit here and do nothing when you could have done so much. You are better than that," said Brandon.

Aaron shook his head, turning in frustration. "I'm really not, Brandon."

Brandon was not moved. "I know you are. And so does Shawna."

Aaron twirled back around. “If that were true then how come she dumped my ass?”

Brandon answered without hesitance. “Because she saw what you were capable of, what you could be before you decided to take things for granted. And when you stopped that, she had no choice but to let you go.”

“Your opinion,” mumbled Aaron.

“If only,” said Brandon, pressing forward. “She’s out there somewhere. And she might just need you now more than ever. I think it’s time you showed her and the whole world what you are really fucking made of.”

Aaron chuckled bitterly before looking at his brother again. “If you knew me half as well as you think you did, you would know that ain’t me,” he countered.

“And if you knew you half as well as I know you, then you’d know I’m right, as per usual,” countered Brandon.

Aaron shook his head as he waved his hand to perish the thought. “No. No, this is me. And I am the fuck out of here,” he said before heading to find the rear exit.

Brandon watched him go, pained to see his brother take the easy route yet again. He wanted nothing more than for Aaron to see his own worth and shine. He had lit a resounding and metaphorical fire under his brother’s ass, but to no avail. At last, Brandon nodded and rested against a nearby counter, lost in thought.

“For what it’s worth, I thought it was a great damn speech,” offered Ron.

“Thanks, Ron,” said Brandon distantly.

“Though I think you could have put a little stink on it and really landed the ending a bit better. I was pretty riveted up to that point though.”

Brandon sunk his head. “God damnit, Ron,” he whispered as he rubbed at his temples.

David looked about the group before watching some of the carnage passing by outside of the store. “What we going to do now, man? I cannot die here. The mamacitas, they need me. They need the much dick. They need the love of David,” he said sagely. And for those counting, it was pronounced Daveed.

Brandon nodded to himself. “Cliff’s right. We must fight. One way or the other, that’s just what we have to do,” he said as he smiled at Cliff. “It’s your mall after all.”

“You’re goddamn right,” said Cliff, standing now. “We are in this together. And we are in this to the end. Who’s with me?”

Ron put a hand in the center of the group quickly. “I’m in.”

Michael joined with a hand of his own. “Same here.”

Dennis added his hand to the mix. “You know I’m not going anywhere.”

David approached and placed his hand atop of Dennis’s. “Me too, gringos,” he said.

“God, I hope you washed that hand, Mr. Much Dick,” mumbled Dennis.

Brandon nodded. “I’ve known you guys for a while. And I can say without a shadow of a doubt that you are some of the best damn people I know.” He placed his hand on top of David’s. “I am with you all the way.”

“Good,” said Cliff with a sage-like smile. “Then let’s do everything we can to see another sunrise together,” he said before placing a bloody hand on top of Brandon’s.

“Aw, fucking fuck all,” said Brandon as he passed out yet again.

“We are going to have to do something about that,” said Michael as the group looked upon Brandon’s unconscious body. "Sure thing," said Ron with a grin and a wink. "As soon as that shit stops being funny."

God damnit, Ron

11

THE DOUCHEMAN COMETH

Through the chaos and unfolding fuckery of his mall, Douglas Whitworth watched casually with cold aloofness. He certainly didn't like the loss of profits he was witnessing, yet somehow recent events had changed his perspective. He was a predator now, offered god-like powers that he deserved. The world was going to hell in a handbag and he already was fashioning plans to be a king.

Despite gorging on his employees, Douglas was still hungry in a manner of speaking. Blood covered his dress shirt and jacket, yet he gave no flying fucks about it. He watched the carnage with revitalized senses, as if he were seeing everything for the first time in his life. Humans ran in hysteria, chased by beings that reeked of death. He paid them little mind though, for from the looks of them they were still much lower on the food chain than him.

Douglas was indeed transformed, but the transformation had done a number on him. His skin now was stone pale and offered an inhuman durability. The remnants of his hair, forgotten thanks to his new abilities, stood mostly on end atop his balding scalp. His girth remained, though it did not bounce as it once did. A spot of blood dribbled down his chin from his new fangs. He now resembled a being sculpted from marble by an artist that was just looking to squeak by with a D for the semester.

As Douglas walked, one of the undead creatures ceased his pursuit of a fleeing woman and instead charged at the easier target. Douglas paid the creature little mind, sensing it as it neared. Reaching out with one hand, Douglas grabbed it by the head, applying pressure to its temples as he lowered the creature to the ground. Soon the head crushed like an overripe melon and Douglas continued his walk, wiping the blood and head bits on his business coat.

Douglas paused then, taking a moment to look down at the creature he had just felled. He had killed it as if it were nothing, had not even given it a single thought. The revelation turned him on a bit. That coupled with the fact that his wanger hadn't been this hard since, well like ever, he was euphoric. He would need some intense negotiations again very, very soon. But first, first he would need a snack or two.

"This is…glorious," said Douglas with pompous nonchalance. "A gift, long overdue. I am who I am supposed to be."

A curvy woman in her early forties caught Mr. Whitmore's eye. She was running right for him, tears streaming down her cheeks as she continued screaming. Behind her two bloody creatures gave chase hungrily. With his acute senses, it was like a Baywatch run. Douglas focused on the woman's shapely breasts as they danced while she fled. She clearly needed help. Douglas snapped himself out of his stare as he motioned for her to come to him.

As the woman threw her arms around Douglas, the mall owner gave both approaching zombies harrowing bitch-slaps, sending their heads flying. The two bodies ran past him several steps before they realized they were missing a crucial part and fell to the ground. The woman cried gratefully in Douglas's arms. He could feel her breasts press against him, accentuated by her heaving sobs.

"Thank you, sir. Thank you so much," she breathed.

"Oh, don't worry," said Douglas smelling her hair like the pervert he was. "You can make it up to me right now." He then whipped her around, cupped her breasts, and bit her neck.

The woman screamed, but it didn't matter to Douglas. The fat man's eyes were rolled up as he savored the blood gushing into his mouth. He fed and pressed against the dying woman like the inconsiderate asshole he was, all the way up until there was no life left in her. He finished about the time she was finished, discarding her as he strutted on unapologetically with new stains on his shirt and pants. For while he was now a supernatural creature of the night, he was still a premature ejaculator.

"More," he croaked ravenously, like the gluttonous, spoiled, fat bastard that he was. "I need more." He then began to amble after more prey, thundering along half-cocked at the teeth and the crotch.

Douglas floundered about then, looking absolutely ridiculous but bolstered by his newfound power. He caught women as they fled, feeding on them savagely while taking time to be all sorts of inappropes. Douglas began to take his time, savoring each feast as he found it. It was liberating knowing he no longer needed money or leverage to get what he wanted.

As he continued his self-gratifying hunt, Douglas came to a grinding halt. He quickly fixed his eyes on prey he'd been hunting for some time now. The vivacious women haunted his naughty thoughts and had filled his camera monitors whenever he could hone-in on her location. Her curves, features, and scent were only increased now thanks to Douglas's heightened senses. At the sight of her, his chubby returned, pointing as if to say, "That's the one, that's the one!"

There, in front of a swanky clothing store, swinging a bloody mannequin arm like a ball bat, was Shawna. She was sweating at the exertion of defending herself and that somehow made her even more alluring to Douglas. He watched her intently, poised like an overweight tiger. Shawna had just finished felling a zombie before standing atop of it and beating it within an inch of its unlife.

Douglas shot in then like a dart, scooping Shawna up and pressing her against the wall. His extra wide, now solid girth pressed up against Shawna as she struggled against him. Douglas smiled, emboldened by the freedom offered by his newfound power. Shawn struck at him and cursed, because it was like punching a waterbed full of concrete. This of course aroused Douglas too, the fat, twisted fuck.

"At last, you are mine," said Douglas, offering her a smile laced with fangs and blood.

"The fuck I am," growled Shawna as she tried to push him away.

"That was far from a request," said Douglas, savoring the struggle and the hunt. He used to have to worry about putting off rapey vibes but those days were long gone now.

Shawna put her hands around his threat, refusing to take an inch of his crap. "If you don't fucking let go of me right fucking now, your shriveled testicles are going on some earrings you'll have to shit out before you can wear them," responded Shawna.

Douglas smiled more deeply, pressing up against Shawna even more. She didn't know whether to be more pissed or gag. "I don't think so, my sweet. I've waited far too long for this moment," he purred.

"Then wait some more, dicknuts," exclaimed a voice.

Shawna sought out the voice. "Aaron?"

To his astonishment, Douglas found himself hurled backwards by an unseen force. He whined and wailed as he was hurled like a Ricky Vaughn fastball into a wall. The floor trembled at the impact as Douglas was embedded into the wall. Shawna fell to the ground, catching her breath and grateful to be free of the girth constricting her.

Rushing to Shawna Aaron helped her back to her feet. "What the fuck was that all about? You okay?"

Shawna brushed him off as she looked angrily back in the direction Douglas had just been tossed. "I'm fucking fine," she spat as she clenched her fists. "I had it under control."

Aaron stifled his frustration as he tried to keep it cool. "I'm sure you did, but I am not gonna sit back and watch some fat fuck try to dry hump or raw dog you during a zombie apocalypse," he said as he looked back at the broken wall. "Was that Mr. Whitmore?"

Shawna growled, still looking at the crumbling wall herself. "Looked like him, but somehow worse. He was like hitting stone. Creepy as fuck stone but stone regardless. He's…changed."

"Well this day just keeps getting better by the god damn minute," said Aaron as he looked about. "I think we better hightail it on out of here now."

"I'm not going anywhere with you," said Shawna.

Aaron ran both of his hands across his face trying to keep his shit refined. "Look, you can still be pissed at me. I can live with that. But there is no way in hell I'm leaving you alone in this shit of a storm."

"Oh, now you want to be chivalrous and romantic," countered Shawna. "Or are you just wanting to get back to your god damn video games?"

Aaron now felt the situation was more than happy to take a metaphorical dump all over his patience. "For fuck's sake, Shawna! I am a dick, I get it, but I fucking love you! Can we deal with this when we get someplace that assholes aren't trying to eat or fuck us?"

Shawna turned her fury down a few notches before replying. "I guess that's fair," she offered.

"Thanks," mumbled Aaron before he used his power to hurl another advancing zombie pinball style between a cluster of trashcans and dishing him into a nearby fountain.

"I see the vaccine did a number on you as well," said Shawna casually.

Aaron nodded. "From the looks of some of the fuckers trying to kill us, I'd say I got lucky," he replied.

"Care to explain what you did to my boyfriend then?"

Aaron shrugged. "We just came to an agreement. Let's not screw the pooch of this momentous occasion with needless details."

"Oh, shit," said Shawna, looking over Aaron's shoulder.

"What?"

"You've pissed him off now," she offered, pointing at the crumbling hole in the wall.

Aaron turned in time to see Mr. Whitworth emerging from the hole he had put the man through. Mr. Whitworth's suit was battered from the forced entry, and his belly was now exposed. His scant hair was in worse shape than before as it gave up any semblance of order. Mr. Whitworth became fixated upon Aaron as he prepared to strike once more.

Aaron waved a hand before him, indicating to Mr. Whitworth to slow his fucking roll. "I think it's time we both chilled out while you kindly fuck off," he said.

"That's it, sweet talk him," mumbled Shawna.

"Trying to," said Aaron, obviously oblivious to his shitty skills at mediation.

"You dare lay your hands on a god?" spat Mr. Whitworth.

"God of what, buffets?" asked Aaron.

"Christ," said Shawna.

Mr. Whitworth snarled as he charged toward Aaron. His strength cracked the ground beneath him as he ambled, hands outstretched. Despite his girth, the man was swift, and the speed caught Aaron by surprise. Aaron recovered and held out his hands, using his power to try to stop the approaching vampire.

Aaron's power hit Mr. Whitworth fully, nearly halting the vampire in his tracks. Grunting, Mr. Whitworth plodded forward with shaky, slow steps. The opposing strengths fought one another as the floor trembled at the display. Aaron began to sweat and strain under the exertion as he realized he could not fully halt the vampire who was using his strength to stand firm like a tree.

"Shawna, you might want to run now," said Aaron through his clenched teeth. "This fucker will do worse to you than me," he said, hinting at more carnal desires than blood.

"Maybe not," said Shawna. "He might not be picky."

"Fucking hell. Thanks for the visual," said Aaron as he pushed his power to the limits.

Mr. Whitworth almost was in reach of Aaron as a smile formed on his face. "You're mine, you little shit," he said.

"Not…into…dudes," strained Aaron, still fighting the vampire's advance.

"Won't matter soon enough," said Mr. Whitworth.

"Fuck all this," said Shawna angrily as she put herself between Aaron and Whitworth.

"Shawna!" screamed Aaron.

Before he could respond, Shawna held up a hand as Mr. Whitworth watched her. Suddenly, the hand emitted a searing flame that engulfed her arm almost to the elbow. Shawna then swung her arm between Mr. Whitworth's legs, grabbing hold of the man's crotch with fire. Mr. Whitworth gasped as his jaw dropped. Despite his powers, he felt the full, heated assault upon his wang.

"Fucking truly, madly, and deeply fuck all the way off," said Shawna before she released Mr. Whitworth's weinie and thrust her hands upon his face.

Igniting her hands again, Shawna covered Mr. Whitworth's entire head and face into a roaring flame. The fat man flailed, torn between covering his face and his crotch. Aaron watched in utter holy fuck all amazement before he remembered where he was. Extending his hands again, he used his powers to hurl the distracted Mr. Whitworth halfway across the mall. The large man flew like a flailing cannonball, doing his best to extinguish his burning face and dong.

With him taken care of, Aaron looked at Shawna, dumbfounded and chock full of questions. "What in all the ass?"

"Long story," she offered before grabbing his hand. "Let's go before he comes back!"

Shawna led Aaron through the chaotic mall, avoiding clutter and corpses as they searched for safety. The zombies were still coming, each wave looking more pissed off than the last. Both Shawn and Aaron used their powers to remain safe as they flung and fried any undead minion foolhardy enough to try and place them on the menu. Finally, Shawna lead them to the scented boutique. Breezing past candles, lotions, and the like, they entered the office in the back before Shawna slammed and locked the door.

"It's an absolute shit show out there," breathed Shawna as she caught her breath.

"You said it," said Aaron, trying absently not to focus on her heaving chest as he too gulped in the air.

Shawna looked down at her hands, the ones she had used to flambé Mr. Whitworth's face and schlong. "So, about that long story," she offered.

"Omega Vaccine?"

"Well, damn, it wasn't as long as I thought it would be," she said

"That's not what she said," he said, with a grin.

"Guess again," she said.

"Hey!" Aaron then tried to ignore the jab by listening through the door. "It's not getting any better out there," he added.

"I wonder how Matt is holding up," said Shawna.

Aaron snorted. "Fuck him. I mean, not literally. You shouldn't be fucking him. And I never would, for the record. Guy's a douche."

"Well at least he makes an effort," said Shawna.

Aaron turned from the door. "Effort? Why isn't he here then? I haven't seen him since he penguined it the fuck outta the mall earlier after looking like he just shit himself in the can," he said.

Shawn's eyes flared as she pointed at Aaron. The tip of her pointed finger began to smoke. "I knew you had something to do with him leaving! You just couldn't leave me the hell alone or accept that we're through!"

Aaron inched closer to her, redirected her finger to avoid having his nuts roasted, so to speak. "Hey, he came at me and threatened me. It's not my fault he's insecure as fuck or that you had to pick a complete asshat to replace me."

"Most things are an upgrade after you," spat Shawna.

"That's just fucking cold. I apologized for the shit I did and for how I fucked up and you still have me doing time for it!" countered Aaron.

"Words are just words, you ass," replied Shawna.

Aaron threw his hands up completely. "Well they sure as shit are when you never let me prove myself! I think you just found it fucking easier to run away than face the feels!"

Shawna slapped him. "You asshole!"

"Unforgiving shrew!" lashed back Aaron.

She tried to slap him again. Aaron caught her hand. "Selfish prick!"

Aaron put an accusing finger right into her face. "Yeah, you know what? I'm gonna fucking give you that one," he said before he threw his arms around her and kissed her deeply.

Shawna pulled her head away, after a moment. "What do you think you are doing?"

"Loving you, cause I fucking love you, okay?" replied Aaron as he kissed her again.

Shawna struck out at him as she resisted. But instead of pulling her head back she fought back with furious kisses. Aaron spanked her once and held on as she lifted her legs and wrapped them around him. Aaron then pressed her up against the nearest wall as they continued a feverish dueling of the tongues. Aaron lost himself in the kiss as he pressed against Shawna completely.

Taking a moment to catch his breath, Aaron marveled at Shawna. "Fuck I missed you."

Though her eyes were filled with desire, Shawna was still firm in her stance. “I’m still pissed at you.”

Aaron nodded. “Good, then you can be on top and have your way with me,” he said before falling on his back before resuming the passionate kissing exchange.

The two of them did the hunka-dunka then, and it was more intense, passionate, angry, and lustful then either of them had ever experienced in their lives. And the sounds that were made in those fiery moments were enough to even keep the zombies away out of either respect or fear.

12

TIME TO ASSEMBLE…SORTA

Sitting in the relative safety of his place of employment, Brandon waited with those that remained. The sounds of carnage were dying down outside, yet this brought him and the others little comfort. Everyone knew the time was coming to venture out and face the world again, but none of them knew what to expect anymore. Brandon knew that it was going to be ugly and bloody and everyone was quickly discovering how he handled bloody, and it was ugly.

Brandon, Cliff, David, and Jim were keeping an eye on Randal, who looked to be having fitful, feverish dreams. The wannabe zombie slayer was looking worse by the hour and the group was still deciding what could be done with him. Right now, all they could do was watch him and wait for the others to return from the back hallways with gear they had stowed away from the custodians' locker room.

Breaking the chaotic monotony that was unfolding outside of the store, Cliff cleared his throat and focused on Brandon. "How are you holding up over there?" he asked.

Brandon offered a brave smile. "Better than I was, thanks," he offered before pointing at Randal. "And a damn sight better than him, I wager."

"Indeed," offered Cliff sagaciously. For as long as Brandon had known him, the custodian had always managed to be cool as fuck no matter the circumstances. "No way of knowing what to expect with him now. We'll take it as it comes."

"You know, he might be turning into a zombie as we speak," offered Brandon.

"The thought has occurred to me, yes," said Cliff.

"Course, after seeing my friends and my brother, he could be turning into something completely different as well."

"I guess I hadn't considered that yet," replied Cliff as he looked on the restless Randal in a new light.

"We could, you know, kick his ass," offered David.

"I don't think that is necessary right now, David, thank you," replied Brandon.

"It would be fun though. He's an asshole."

"As tempting as it would be, let's play it cool for now, amigo," offered Brandon.

"If you say so," replied David, disappointment evident at the missed opportunity of ass kicking.

Brandon thought about his next words before speaking again. "You know, I am not saying we should kill him, cause we sure don't know how this is going to pan out, but maybe we should restrain him a bit, just in case."

"A fair point," said Cliff as he called out to Jim behind the counter. "Jim, you have any duct tape handy?"

"Plain or themed?" asked Jim.

Cliff shrugged. “Ah, what the hell. How about themed? Might as well add some color to this day. Surprise me.”

“On my way,” said Jim.

Jim brought over a cluster of themed duct tapes. Brandon and Cliff agreed on Marvel and bound Randal’s wrists and ankles. As an afterthought, Brandon nabbed the Batman duct tape and covered Randal’s mouth. He, like Cliff, leaned toward Marvel over D/C, but Brandon was all for being an equal opportunity nerd. Satisfied, the two friends continued their vigil as they anxiously awaited the return of their comrades and friends.

As they were finishing their work, an alarm blared through the entire mall for several seconds. Brandon and the others stood, alert at the sudden change. Exchanging glances, the group debated on what to do when the alarms stopped as suddenly as they started. Before they could be relieved for their ears though, a voice filled the speakers throughout the mall. It was the grating voice of Douglas Whitworth, the mall owner. Everyone knew the voice quite well, and all would have rather gladly cleaned their urethra’s out with sandpaper than deal with the man.

Pompously, the mall owner spoke. “To the survivors of my mall, this is Douglas Whitworth, owner and operator of this establishment. I have initiated a lock down of my building so that no one gets in or out. With recent…changes that have transpired, I have decided to implement a new order. That being stated, all survivors within the mall will have the opportunity to pledge loyalty to me. Those that oppose this new rule shall be food and fodder to further the cause. That is all, for now," said Mr. Whitworth before the intercom went silent once more.

Brandon rolled his eyes. “Welcome to fucking Thunderdome,” he muttered.

"I always hated that fuck," said Cliff.

"He sounds different," mused David. "Cocky, even for him."

Brandon let a slow facepalm cover his features. "He's probably a vampire now or some shit," he replied dejectedly. "No way he would be that casual or bold without something up his sleeve."

"Well," started Cliff musing. "If we want out of this nightmare, we are going to have to face him and whatever monster he has become."

"Point of order," said Brandon holding up a finger. "He was always a monster as a human being. I am sure whatever he has morphed into hasn't helped his disposition in the slightest."

"A pinche' grande dickhead," offered David.

"Most likely," offered Brandon.

"I don't mean to be a buzzkill, but we are going to need weaponry to survive," said Jim, still watching Randal warily.

Cliff nodded. "The boys will be back soon," he replied.

Brandon smiled. "And it's not like we don't have a few things here, boss. I know you have some goodies in the back, swords especially."

"Mint in box," said Jim proudly and defensively.

"I think all values got shot to shit about an hour or so ago," replied Brandon. "Best we worry about surviving for the time being. You could be telling us it's dangerous to go alone, so take this with you and what not."

Jim instantly picked up on the Legend of Zelda reference. "You calling me old?"

"Never to your face," replied Brandon grinning. "But I think you have earned the right to not be on the front lines of the upcoming fight."

"Fair enough. I'll go round up the best of what I got," said Jim sadly as he set about to his work.

Brandon and the others watched him go before they were distracted by the sound of a door opening. Cliff held his newly acquired pistol at the ready, but was relieved to see that it was the rest of his crew returned. Ron, Michael, and Dennis each carried duffle bags laden with equipment. Putting the bags down, the three men caught their breath as Cliff began to evaluate their cache of stuff.

"Sorry it took so long, boss," said Ron as he patted one of the duffel bags. "But we had to make an extra trip for the bags. It's a real shit show out there."

"You made it back safely. That's what matters," said Cliff as he started unzipping bags and procuring the contents.

Brandon watched as the group emptied the bags of their contents. Between the trigger-happy jocks gear and the accumulated items the custodians had acquired over the years, he was surprised to see a smorgasbord of makeshift and honest to god weapons of ass-kicking. Guns, knives, bows, swords and the like now littered the floor as the group decided what they would arm themselves with. A 13-inch dildo also fell from one of the bags. Dennis kicked it aside, mumbling something about anything could be used as a weapon under the proper circumstances.

Brandon watched as Michael silently procured his chosen gear while the others sifted still through the weaponry. He secured two 9mm Glocks with flashlights attached with leg holsters and extra ammo clips. On his belt he added extendable batons and on his new pack he slung on two hand axes and a lever action hunting rifle with a scope. Thus geared, Michael completed his look with a compound hunting bow and quiver of arrows.

As Michael finished, Dennis had finally found what he needed. He had gotten hold of the AR-15 and now kissed the rifle affectionately. Grabbing all the clips he could for it, Dennis then put on a shoulder holster for a .357 Magnum. He then grabbed a ball bat that had a table saw blade put through the top, making it look like one mean, motherfucking axe. He gave a wink to Brandon as he attached the bat and two old plumbers wrenches to his pack.

"Ya'll, I think I'm in love," cooed Ron as he pulled a prize from one of the duffel bags. Holding it before him, Ron ogled over a SAP-6 shotgun, a sleek, light weapon with a magazine, scope, and flashlight. He patted it proudly as if it were a new friend and continued to look like a kid at Christmas.

"You plan on sharing?" asked Dennis.

"You know shotguns are my thing. You find another damn thing," said Ron as he pulled the bag with the shotguns closer. He then pointed at the dildo Dennis had kicked away earlier. "In fact, there's a thing right there, use that."

"I can't use that on a zombie," countered Dennis.

"Yeah, but if you think you are getting this shotgun you can use it to go fuck yourself," said Ron.

"Kinky," said Dennis with a grin. "I knew there was a reason I loved you."

"Hell, I love you too, but the shotgun clause stands," said Ron.

"Fine," muttered Dennis.

Happy, Ron brought out a tactical shotgun, a Beretta 9-millimeter, a sawed-off shotgun, and a belt of shotgun shells. Slinging the tactical shotgun to his pack, he added a machete as well as a sledgehammer. The Beretta and sawed-off went in leg holsters as he proudly double-checked his gear.

"Show-off," said Dennis.

"Salty heifer," said Ron affectionately.

"I hope you two are quite finished," said Cliff as he turned about to look at them. Michael gave an approving nod as Ron and Cliff whistled.

Cliff, from his legs, under his armpits, belt, and chest was carrying seven holstered pistols. On his pack was a massive sword known as Frostmourne, a replica from the game World of Warcraft as well as a military shovel and flares. Brandon thought the sword was a nice touch, elegantly keeping to nerd roots while also proudly stating "I am not one whom you want to fuck with."

"Well, it looks like you have the kick ass part down well. All you need now is the bubblegum," observed Brandon.

"Shit, I knew we forgot something," said Dennis.

"This is why you don't get no shotguns," offered Ron.

Cliff then looked between Brandon and David. "What about you two?"

"Well I was waiting on you guys to finish having your fun," said Brandon.

And David patted his groin region proudly. "I'm good, man," he stated proudly.

Cliff shook his head. "Well as happy as I am in your own confidence, I insist that you take something with you. You know, to put my mind at ease."

"Try this," said Michael as he tossed a sheathed katana to David.

David drew the blade. "I don't know, man," he offered, looking at the blade with extreme scrutiny.

"Think of it as an extension of your penis," said Brandon.

"Like your penis went Super Saiyan or something," added Ron.

David put the blade back in its scabbard as he nodded. “I can live with that,” he said before slinging the blade onto his back.

“And as for you,” said Cliff as he sized up Brandon.

“I think with my current issues with blood I would be better suited for ranged attacks,” mused Brandon in all honesty.

“Try this one,” said Ron as he tossed Brandon a holstered firearm.

Catching it, Brandon pulled the weapon from its holster, looking upon a compact Taurus PT111. Brandon held it carefully, not wanting to drop it and look like a total dipshit among his compadres. The gun was easy to hold, and the holster had a clip for his belt. Brandon put the holster at his hip before putting the gun away.

Ron handed him a handful of clips. “That should be easy for you to handle and the clip holds 13 rounds, so it should serve you well enough in a pinch,” he said.

“Thanks, Ron,” said Brandon.

“Course if the zombies get ya or you find yourself covered in a blood bath, best keep a round to do yourself in with.”

“God dammit, Ron,” muttered Brandon, for the moment was over pretty damn quickly after that.

“Speaking of that,” said Cliff as procured a pair of tinted sunglasses and handed them to Brandon. “This might help. These glasses will at least make things look black and white. Maybe you can convince yourself you are looking at chocolate syrup and it won’t freeze you up,” said Cliff.

Brandon accepted the glasses gratefully and tried them on, admiring his modified vision. “Well then, this just might work, Cliff. Thank you,” he said before focusing back upon the head custodian. "So, what's the plan?"

Cliff checked two of his handguns one last time before he commented. "Ron, Mike, Dennis, and I will lead the way. Right now, this mall is secured for the most part. We will need to clear it out and establish a base camp until we can figure out how bad things are on the outside. Brandon, David, you two keep close and we will do our best to protect you. If anyone gets into trouble, call it out. Our main objectives are to clear out any remaining zombies and send the owner of this mall straight to hell in a handbasket signed and delivered. Any questions?"

David raised his hand. "I want dibs on any mamacitas we rescue," he said.

Brandon rubbed at one of his temples once more. "It's like that Milli Vanilli song, but instead he blames it on the wang," he said.

Cliff ignored David's request and looked at Jim. "What about you?"

Jim motioned to his store. "This is my ship. I'm it's captain. I'll remain here, even if it means I go down with it."

Cliff nodded. "Once we leave, secure the back door. I want to see you on the other side alive and well," he said.

"Will do," said Jim as he administered a round of handshakes. "I wish you all the best of luck. If you find that sack of shit, you be sure to put a round in him for me."

"You got it," said Cliff as he looked about at the others. "Are we ready?"

"As ready as we are going to be," said Brandon as the others nodded their agreement.

Cliff drew a deep breath and tried to reduce his tension. "Alright then. Jim, open the gate and let us out. Be ready to close it immediately. We'll make sure no one gets in." Jim nodded to this as the group prepared to venture out.

Lifting his head up, Ron looked at Cliff expectantly. "You mind if I lead the charge, boss?"

Cliff raised the two guns in his hands. "I'm right behind you, brother," he replied. "Do us proud and sum us up with it." He nodded to Jim to open the gate.

As the gates slowly opened, the sounds from outside the store became move vivid and haunting. The shrieks of survivors and the hissing rasps of zombies filled their ears. Brandon was immediately grateful for the sunglasses as the carnage was bordering on bloodbath. Michael notched an arrow in his bow as Dennis made sure his rifle was good to go. Cliff drew a calming breath as he waited on Ron's signal, something he hoped would exemplify the group and bolster them as they tried to blaze their way to glory.

Ron then let his voice be heard by all. "Game on, bitches. *Leeroy Jenkins*!!!" he thundered before running into the mall's hallways, SAP-6 shotgun a blazing.

Cliff lowered his head, watching glory present itself briefly before crawling gloriously back up its own ass. "God dammit, Ron," said the group in near unison before charging out to join their friend.

13

HOW REAL THE SHIT BECOMES

The group, led by an enthusiastic Ron, charged from Jim's store, weapon's blazing. At Ron's Warcraft infused battle cry, zombies rushed, attracted to the noise and prospect of fresh flesh. The zombies surged from around corners and from shops, covered in blood and guts and hungry for more. The mall may have been closed off from the outside, but it was still saturated by the undead from within.

Against the approaching storm of collective stiffs and fury, Ron answered first. Using his newly acquired shotgun, he fired methodically, taking heads clean off as he did. Zombies ambled headless and confused a few more steps before falling to the ground. Dennis soon gave him cover fire with his assault rifle, offering controlled bursts either aimed at incoming heads or their legs to slow them down. Cliff offered methodical shots with his handguns as Michael picked his attacks with the bow and arrow.

Pushing forward, Ron and Dennis cut a swath through the pissed off zombies. Cliff and Michael began to cover the rear as Brandon and David hovered at the ready. As one zombie jumped from a hiding place, Brandon turned and shot it in the groin. Instinctively, even though undead, the gnarled, animated corpse grabbed for its cojones just before David cut off its head with his katana. Some blood spatter hit Brandon who did his very best to keep his shit together.

"Just chocolate syrup, just chocolate syrup," he mumbled to himself in a steady mantra.

"You are a weird gringo," stated David.

"So says the man who wished to vanquish the undead with nothing but his schlong," countered Brandon as he fired his gun again.

"Save it for later, we've got bigger issues right now," commanded Cliff.

"They're not bigger than my much dick," said David.

"Save it, David!"

"It is Da-veed!"

"Fucking hell!"

With the way clear, the group pushed forward, reloading their weaponry as they did. Brandon stayed wary as the sounds of hungry zombies and frightened screams still littered the hallways. Cliff and Dennis kept a decent pace as they cleared the main hallway and came toward the food court once more. For moment, the group had time to catch their breaths.

"Ya'll, I don't mind admitting I'm a little turned on right now," said Ron.

"My nipples could currently cut serious glass," agreed Dennis.

"Cliff," said Michael, wanting at least a check to be put on his loveable, yet interesting friends.

"Well, keep it in your pants, folks," ordered Cliff before pointing to his katana-wielding comrade. "And that goes double for you."

"Fucking haters," mused David.

"We're almost to the food court. Let's set up a perimeter and hopefully rest and rehydrate," said Cliff as they turned the corner.

"Oh, holiest of shits," said Brandon as they did.

The group came to an immediate halt as they gawked at the food court. The area was littered with corpses, blood, and bits strewn far and wide. But also, it possessed a cluster of undead feeding on these corpses, most of them laid out on the tables as the zombies casually dined on them. Sure, they were vile creatures who hungered for flesh, but apparently, they didn't want to be savages about it.

And then they turned to gaze hungrily on the fresh meat that had come to them, and all decorum was discarded as they charged with hungry barbarity.

"Fall back, fall the fuck back!" ordered Cliff.

The group didn't have to be told again as they high-tailed it the fuck out of Dodge. Though as they retreated, they noticed another cluster of zombies charging toward them. They fired in all directions as they fled, deciding just what in the hell to do now. Cliff looked about, weighing their options as they ran.

Cliff then pointed to the stairs between them and the rushing zombies. "Head for the stairs! Haul ass!"

The group lost its cohesion as they rushed forward, firing at the rushing zombies to slow them down. In the retreat, Dennis slipped on a pool of blood. Seeing him fall, Michael and David stopped to help him up. The delay was enough to separate them as the others reached the stairs before the zombies did. With the undead horde's attention divided between the separated groups, Michael, Dennis, and David used the distraction to blast their way through the zombies before them while staying ahead of the zombies giving chase. Brandon called out to his friends, but it was too late to do anything but keep fleeing.

The shitstorm continued for the trio as the moved, afraid to stop for anything. Another cluster of brain-munchers forced the group to react. Michael and Dennis veered one way as David ran the other, oblivious in the moment that they were separated from one another. There was no opportunity to rejoin one another as survival trumped all else.

Cut off from the others, Michael and Dennis kept hauling ass.

"I'm too old for this shit," huffed Dennis.

"You're 35," countered Michael.

"Any age is too old for this kind of shit," offered Dennis.

"Fair enough," said Michael.

"What do we do now," wheezed Dennis.

"We have to hole up," offered Michael before pointing to a door marked "employees only." "Let's head back to Jim's."

"Right behind you," breathed Dennis, not wanting to say another damn word and reserve his lungs for breathing.

Reaching the doors, Michael threw them open as Dennis covered them. Both friends entered, slamming the doors shut behind them. Michael held them as Dennis secured the lock. Taking a moment to catch their breaths, the two custodians moved through the employee hallway as the cluster of zombies beat upon the door.

Retracing their steps, the two made their way back to Dabbles and Dorkery, rapping on the door. Within moments, Jim let them in. The two friends collapsed on the ground and reclaimed their breath as Jim secured the door and inspected them. “Are you two alright? Where’s the rest of the group?” he asked.

“Hopefully doing better than we are,” gasped Dennis, happy to be stationary again.

“We got overwhelmed and split up,” said Michael as he jerked a thumb upwards. “They headed to the second floor and we couldn’t keep up. How’s Randal?”

Jim shook his head. “Worse, I’m afraid,” he said, shaking his head. “His fever’s deepened and he’s becoming delirious.”

“He led a gun crazed group of loonies on a fucking shooting spree, I would say delirious comes with the package,” said Dennis.

“Okay, more than normal then,” offered Jim.

Michael and Dennis exchanged glances. “We better go take a look,” said Michael as the two stood up and followed Jim.

Jim’s diagnosis was spot-on. To Michael and Dennis, Randal looked like dogshit. His skin was pale and his breaths where quick and shallow. His muscular arms shivered as his gut quivered. Randal’s patriotic t-shirt was now riddled with sweat. He looked at the three men watching him expectantly, his eyes pleading for help.

“Randal, you aren’t looking so good,” offered Michael softly as he removed the duct tape.

“Course not,” croaked Randal. “I been racked and bit and tossed around. I don’t think you’d be doing much better in my boots,” he replied.

“We’ll give you that,” said Dennis before he looked between Jim and Michael. “What do we do with him?”

Michael shrugged briefly, offering a quick shake of his head. “What can we do with him? There’s nothing in the first aid book about zombie bites,” said Michael.

"We've seen enough movies, though," said Dennis.

"We're not killing him if that's what you mean," said Michael.

"I'm with Mike on this one," said Jim.

"Me too," croaked Randal.

Dennis rolled his eyes, pointing to Randal. "Well that's all fine and dandy, but we should at least knock his ass back out just in case," he said.

"That might be a fair compromise," said Michael.

Dennis nodded before kneeling and procuring the 13-inch dildo. "You hold him, and I'll club him till he goes to sleep."

Redness flared through Randal's face as he growled at the trio. "I have had it with you crazy fuckers. You've been pains in my ass since we met and I'm sick of it. I'm god damn sick with it and I've had enough!" he rumbled before a change washed over him.

Michael, Dennis, and Jim backed away from Randal as the proud gun enthusiast was wracked with convulsions. Foaming slightly from his mouth, Randal's gurgling gasp changed into a ferocious roar. The others were spellbound as Randal's pupils turned yellow and the teeth in his mouth sharpened. Soon his shirt burst open as muscle and fur freed itself from confinement. Within seconds the man had morphed into a bipedal monster as he stood and fixed hungry eyes on the others.

The trio were now looking on a very large, and very pissed off werewolf.

Shaking his head, Dennis tossed the dildo away. "Told you we should have clubbed him," he murmured.

Brandon, Cliff, and Ron rushed quickly up the stairs. The act bought them some time, as some of the zombies in pursuit turned out to not be "stair types." Tripping on the stairs and then other zombies bought the three some valuable distance as they searched frantically for a safe spot. The second floor proved to be less intense, but this made them no less wary of those lurking in wait, searching for a fresh snack.

"Ya'll, this is a bunch of bullshit," wheezed Ron as he put a fresh clip into his SAP-6 shotgun.

"Just keep moving," gasped Cliff. "We need to find a shady spot to lay low."

"We run much longer I'll prolly just have one of ya'll kill me quick," replied Ron.

"Over there," said Brandon, pointing the shop known as Kitchen Zen.

Running to the shop, the three friends rushed inside. Brandon caught his breath as Ron and Cliff grabbed two big trash bins and laid them in front of the door. Brandon caught on and fetched some chairs as the group used odds and ends to fortify the doors. Mostly satisfied, all three of them slumped on the ground and out of sight as they caught their breath.

"Why did you pick this store?" asked Cliff.

Brandon gulped in more air before responding. "One door. Easy to defend. It's got knives and pans and what not. And some food stuffs," said Brandon between breaths.

"You can make me a Bloody Mary," said Ron.

"Shut up, Ron," said Cliff and Brandon simultaneously.

The group then quieted at the roar of a zombie trudging down the hall. Brandon looked up just enough to see outside. A bloodied zombie in a three-piece suit and matted hair sniffed the air as he searched for fresh quarry. His right foot rested at an awkward angle as he limped about hungrily. Soon the zombie passed by the store and the three relaxed a bit.

"I wonder how the others are doing," mused Brandon.

"I'm sure they're fine," said Cliff. "But we should find them soon just to be sure."

"I'm not too fond of our odds," said Brandon as he checked his handgun.

"Well you just gotta look on the bright side, B," offered Ron.

"And what bright side would that be?"

"Well, if we get overrun, lord knows the blood will have you passed out before the eatin' ever starts. You run a chance of being dead before you ever realize it."

"Thanks for that, Ron, really. I think you missed your calling as a motivational speaker," said Brandon coarsely.

"What can I say, when you got the gift, you got the gift," replied Ron.

Brandon stood cautiously before motioning to the store. "Well, I suppose we should find a drink and some snacks. Lord knows when we may have the chance again," he said before pointing to the bar section of the store. "I'll get to work on that drink for you, Ron. Served straight up."

"Much obliged," said Ron.

"Yo ass," added Brandon.

Ron pointed at him as he headed to the snacks. "I'm gonna let you slide on that one, being a Weird Science reference and all."

The three found jerky, cheese, and other snacks as well as water, sodas, and some alcoholic beverages. Ron placed a few of the spirits in his bag for later use as the three comrades recharged. Brandon searched about, looking for things he could use as weapons. A badass looking chef knife caught his eye as well as a culinary torch and a heavy-duty meat tenderizer. He found a way to attach all these items to his belt, feeling a little more secure in protecting himself now.

"I think we should bail as soon as the coast is clear," said Cliff as he looked between his friends. "Thoughts?"

"What do we do until then?" asked Brandon.

"I don't know," said Ron as he held up a pan. "But maybe I will show ya'll how to make some grits and shit," he added in his best impression of Paula Dean.

"By his sunny disposition, you'd never know there was an apocalypse going on," said Brandon.

"Just ever and always a ray of fucking sunshine," stated Cliff.

Just then, the three were drawn to a loud pounding noise at the front of the store. There in the window was the suit toting zombie from before. He bloodied the glass as he pounded upon it, gazing upon the living with a hunger that bordered on horny. The zombie's yelling was drawing others to rally behind his cause.

"I think that's the cue to take the back hallways," said Cliff.

"Right behind you," said Brandon.

As the three headed to the other exit, they heard the door moan before caving in. Soon the sound of more zombies flooded the store as they charged in, ready for humans on the raw. Brandon and his friends now found themselves in the same position as a sex doll thrown into the middle of a Viagra convention.

Fucked.

As they prepared to defend themselves from the incoming zombies, the glass keeping out the zombies at the front door began to crack under the constant pressure.

"So…now what?" asked Brandon.

Ron shrugged as he pumped his shotgun. "Well I hope your flexible and all, brother, cause chances are we're all kissing our own asses goodbye soon. But this ass ain't going down without a fight."

Brandon nodded at him, drawing his firearm and the meat tenderizer. "I'm with you all the way."

Cliff drew two of his handguns before aiming at the incoming zombies from the rear. "Let's show these stiff fucks what we are made of," he commanded before opening fire.

With the zombies at the door still trying to break in, the trio kept their focus on the creatures already within the store. Blood, brains, snacks, and cutlery flew about as bullets lanced through the hungry undead. The fallen corpses slowed the ravenous charge, making it easier to kill the zombies, but it also further entrenched the three friends in the store. Behind them, the glass cracked more, letting them know their safety from that direction was almost at an end.

Procuring loaded pistols, Cliff yelled out orders. "Keep pressing them, Brandon! Ron, cover the front door!"

"There's too many out there to last much longer, man," said Ron reloading his shotgun.

"Then you hang on as long as you got bullets and the will to live!" yelled Cliff.

"Like you gotta tell me twice," Ron hollered back.

Brandon reloaded his handgun, painfully aware that he was down to his last two clips. Soon he would have to fight at close range, and that was not a place he wanted to be at in terms of hungry fuckers wanting to eat him and the potential of blood loads of blood spatter. Aiming his gun again, he set his focus on the nearest zombie head as the glass behind him and his friends finally gave way.

It was then that a unique battle cry filled the mall and drew the zombies' attention up front.

At the sound of that battle cry, Brandon turned his head. "David?"

Sure enough, outside in the hallways and running through the encroaching orgy of zombie flesh was David Roma. In one hand he held to a bloody katana and in the other was a handgun blazing rage into approaching zombies. David hacked and slashed his way through the hallway with a score of zombies on his tail. Despite this, he ran close to the ones assaulting the Kitchen Zen entrance, placing some bullets in some undead skulls as he sliced a few more.

"Suck my much dick, beetches! Vive Da-veed, siempre!" he screamed defiantly as he rushed down the hall. Several of the zombies soon gave chase. The trio inside the shop looked dumfounded for a moment as they processed what had just happened.

"Well scratch my butt, don't that beat all," said Ron.

"Think it's time we took advantage," said Cliff as he shot at the straggling zombies inside the store. "Ron, get us out of here."

"Say no more," said Ron as he blasted open the door.

The three friends ran outside, finishing off the remaining cluster of zombies. From the sound of things, more were alerted to their presence. Cliff looked about before motioning for the others to make their way down the hallway and away from the thick of things. Brandon looked about as they retreated for any sign of David.

He unfortunately found none.

Back at Dabbles and Dorkery, things were looking pretty shitty for Michael, Dennis and Jim. Randal had gone full wolf-shit on them and was doing an exceptional job at expressing his rage. The two custodians had tried reasoning with the werewolf to no avail. With the diplomatic approach shot all sorts to hell, the two realized they would have to resort to more drastic measures as they procured their weapons and prepared for battle.

Seeing that Randal was now looking upon them as if there were nothing more than Purina Dog Chow, Michael shot with his bow while Dennis unloaded a clip from his assault rifle. The bullets either partially sunk into Randal's furry flesh or bounced off completely. The arrow sunk into the werewolf's shoulder but was ripped out quickly before the wound started to immediately heal. These attacks slowed Randal some, but mostly just pissed him off further, much to the dismay of the two custodians.

"Well shit all," said Michael as he exchanged a glance with Dennis before drawing another arrow. "I don't see this ending well."

Dennis put a fresh clip into his assault rifle hastily. "You and I both. And if we die right now, I just wanted you to know, from one heterosexual to another, you've always had an ass I was jealous of."

Michael nodded as he fired again. "Somehow I always had a hunch you felt that way."

And then Randal was upon them. Tucking in his shoulder, the werewolf barreled into both custodians, sending them hurtling over shelves and crashing into other aisles. Randal howled triumphantly then, and it was an exaggerated sound of repressed anger and horniness. Mike and Dennis offered collective groans as they reluctantly pulled themselves off the ground.

"I never signed up for this shit, for the record," said Dennis as he began hurling action figures at Randal as he searched for his assault rifle. Behind the counter, Jim expressed his disgust of such an endeavor.

"You know we all got into this job for the action," replied Mike as he brandished one of his machetes and his sidearm.

"Now let's show this harry sack of shitballs how we clean house." He then opened fire on Randal again.

"I thought it was for the ladies," said Dennis as he found and grabbed his assault rifle.

Both friends fired on Randal with all that they had, receiving more frustrating results. Randal seemed only to be more pissed than he was moments before. The werewolf now looked between the aisles at Michael and Dennis, as if deciding on who he should kill first. At last he fixed on Dennis, determining that the assault rifle was more annoying than a customer coming in at 9:59 when closing time is 10.

Dennis continued firing as he slowly retreated. Randal upended a section of comics to reach him. "If you have any bright ideas, I feel like now would be a great fucking time to share them, Mike!"

"Hold on," said Mike as he searched the shelves. Seeing what he wanted, Mike grabbed a ball and held it up for Randal. "Here, boy! Fetch!" he offered before tossing the ball. Randal watched it as it flew before turning an impatient glance in Michael's direction. He then returned his attention to Dennis.

"What the fuck, man?" bellowed Dennis.

"It was worth a shot, alright?" said Mike as he looked around the shop, hoping for some inspiration. Nothing was working on Randal and Dennis was just seconds away from being a chew toy. Casting his glance over the movie section, he was quickly reminded of an old 80's classic that revealed a crucial bit of information regarding the monster world.

The wolfman's got nards.

Inspiration hit Michael quickly. "Keep him occupied! I've got an idea!" he exclaimed.

Dennis unloaded another clip as Randal inched closer and closer. "Feed the fucker! Scratch his belly! Let him hump your leg, but for shit's sake, don't let him eat or fuck me!"

Michael then ran down the aisle away from Randal and his friend. Leaping over the display of DVD's, he placed himself behind Randal. The werewolf was just about on his friend now. Running toward them, Mike dove forward and twisted as he drew close. Landing on his back, the bearded custodian slid between Randal's legs, coming to a stop underneath him. As Randal looked down, he saw as Mike placed his machete blade and gun barrel upon his testicles. Randal's eyes widened, and the action sent his ferocity to a grinding halt.

"Ruh-roh," said Randle, as he lowered his arms and calmed himself.

Dennis lowered his assault rifle, relieved to be alive. "Nice thinking, bro. I guess he don't want to get neutered after all."

Mike nodded confidently, though he didn't favor where he now found himself. "See? He can still see reason. I take it you understand me just fine, don't you, Randy?"

The werewolf growled but nodded his head. "Ruh-huh."

"Good," offered Mike as he grinned. "So, what we are going to do now is make the most of this event and turn a negative into a positive," he said before motioning with his head. "Dennis, would you grab me some twine and a grenade? I think it's time to fashion a leash."

Randal's eyes narrowed. "Ro Rway rou reash my reck, rasshole," he uttered defiantly.

Michael's grin deepened. "Oh, they are not going around your neck, douchetard," he said merrily. Suddenly, Dennis perked up as he caught on.

Randal lowered his head and shoulders in defeat. "Rudderrucker," he grumbled at the revelation.

Laying against a wall, on the floor in the men's bathroom, David Roma fought hard to catch his breath. Before him was a trail of dead zombies. His gun, empty of bullets, rested in his right hand. The remnants of his broken katana were lodged in the head of a zombie he killed before retreating into the shitter. David was totally spent. It had been one hell of a fight and he had sent every last one of the zombies on his tail straight to hell.

Still struggling for breath, David reflected on what had just transpired. He had unleashed hell and fury on a bunch of dead hombres, and despite being outnumbered, he had come out on top. Now he was feeling bittersweet about the whole affair, for while he was victorious, no beautiful women saw his miraculous exploits. Had this been a different situation, such bravado and machismo would have gotten him laid at least a handful of times.

Pulling himself to his knees, David turned on the water faucet on the bathroom sink. Splashing cool water on his face, David cherished the feeling before drinking heavily, grateful for the liquid that filled his throat. Satisfied, he gasped for more air, letting the coolness of the water calm him further. David hoped his friends in the Zen Kitchen made it out alright. And if they did, they owed him big time.

With his breath reclaimed, David listened intently to the halls outside of the bathroom. He scratched at his wispy mustache, contemplating his next move. He could hear sounds of an ensuing battle, along with zombie howls, growing fainter as the fight was drawing away from him. This gave him some peace, for he desperately needed more weaponry if he were to get back to kicking ass.

Satisfied the coast was mostly clear, David regained his feet. Taking a moment, he looked himself over in the mirror, pleased with what he saw. Sure, he was covered with blood, sweat, and brain bits, but it gave him a manly flair in his opinion, a rugged machismo if you will. All he had to do now was find a mamacita in distress and maybe some Coronas, then he could call it a bitching end to a shit day.

"You did good, man," he said to his reflection proudly. "Cause you the man, man."

David then turned from the mirror and lost his cocky grin. Instantly his ears were filled with the sounds of someone sniffing like a bloodhound. Soon a zombie entered the bathroom, attracted to his scent. Her eyes set upon him and she hissed hungrily. The predator had locked eyes on its prey and was ready to feed.

David's eyes widened in recognition of the zombie. "Janette?" he breathed.

A snarl met David in reply as Janette eyed him hungrily. There was anger in her eyes as she bared blood-stained teeth. Her jeans, blonde hair, and blue shirt were also covered in a concoction of bodily fluids and gunk. Her tattered shirt held two bullet holes at her waist and was inches away from fully revealing her left breast. David could not help but focus on that as Janette noticed the fallen zombies that lead to David.

David held a hand forward, hoping to reason with his turned friend. "Now wait a minute, mamacita. You had a bad day. David is still your friend."

"David," snarled Janette.

He shook his head. "No, Da-veed," he replied casually. Another snarl made him hold up both his hands. "Okay, we talk on that later. But please, keep calm, for there is no need to fight. I cannot kill a mamacita like you."

"Feed," uttered Janette as she pointed to him.

David shook his head, still trying to keep things chill. “No, baby. Not like that. I wanted to take you to eat. Not eat me. Don’t be like that. Let David love you.”

“Feed!” Janette repeated.

At this, David lowered his arms and nodded sagely. “I cannot change your mind and I cannot kill you,” he said as his eyes swelled with determination. He then unzipped his pants proudly. “I will either fuck the evil from you or die trying. Come to your papi, mamacita.”

As he motioned for Janette to approach, the zombie obliged, running with her arms outstretched. David screamed defiantly as he rushed her, somehow scared and courageous and fully erect. From outside the bathroom, the sounds that could be heard where a crescendo of crashes, grunts, moans, and screams of pleasure and pain. Even zombies drawn to the sound dared not venture into that men’s room and sought their food elsewhere.

It was a struggle that lasted for nearly half an hour before silence covered the bathroom completely and the legend of David Roma truly began.

Free of the Zen Kitchen, Brandon, Cliff, and Ron battled their way through the hallway. Tired as they were, the three friends were bolstered for the moment at least, for they were no longer trapped between a rock and a hard place. Brandon could still feel the grimness exuding from Cliff though, as the man must have been thinking and feeling the same as Brandon. They were all getting low on ammo.

Clearing another corner, the group came across another band of undead hell bent on brain chow. Ron let his opposing opinion on the matter be spoken with his shotguns, clearing a clip as he mowed down all six of the baddies himself.

Shaking his head, he reloaded his shotgun angrily. “Christ’s sake on a cracker, how much more do we gotta contend with?” he muttered.

Cliff checked his own ammo as he replied. “They are still getting in somehow. We’ve gotta figure out where that is and close it off,” he stated.

“Food court is likely cleared now,” breathed Brandon as he kept up. “Let’s start there.”

The trio made it the rest of the way without incident. The group was relieved to see that Brandon was right and the court was indeed clear of all but one zombie. Ron was more than happy to sneak up on it and beat the tar out of it as it fed to keep things quiet. The group then checked to see if the coast was clear before heading to the doors.

“There it is,” said Brandon, pointing to the breach. While the security barriers were in fact down, one of them was being propped open by a table. From the looks of it, some people had tried to escape only to meet their makers by the influx of zombies.

“Well, let’s hop to it then,” said Ron as he approached the door.

The table proved to be a certifiable pain in the ass lodged in the door as it was. Brandon did his best to pull on it as Ron pushed from the other side. Cliff had two of his handguns procured and was doing his best to cover both of their asses as he watched for zombies. Silently Cliff willed for their success as he crouched and continued to scan their surroundings.

"Holy shits snacks on wheat toast, a stubborn Alabama tick don't have anything on this table," growled Ron through gritted teeth.

"I'll take your word for it," replied Brandon through the strain.

"Just keep pushing, guys. We need this door closed before we have to deal with more assholes than we've got bullets for," said Cliff.

Ron nodded despite the strain of pushing. "Yup. Then we get some food. Then we figure all this shit out."

"I could stand to eat," said Brandon. "And after that I want to sleep for about 2 years. And then...shit."

"Yeah you would want to do that after all that eating and sleeping. Comes pretty naturally," said Ron from the other side of the barrier.

"No, man. We've got some company," said Brandon, looking over his shoulder.

Standing again, Cliff trained his guns on two rushing zombies, being careful with his aim. Busting the proverbial caps in their asses, Cliff hit both zombies in the head. As they fell, he approached them, checking to see if there were truly dusted. Cliff then looked about the food court, seeing if his commotion had attracted any more of the undead. Relieved that it had not, Cliff turned and made his way back to the doors.

And then shit got way too real.

From behind the counter of the tacky frozen yogurt shop, a ravenous turned employee leapt upon Cliff. The custodian was caught off guard as he was tackled to the ground, losing one of his guns in the process. Holding the gnarled, bloody zombie with his now free hand, he fired shots into its stomach, trying to get his gun up to its head. Cliff felt his gun run empty after three shots. Swearing to himself, Cliff finally got the gun up and jammed it into the zombie's mouth. The zombie chomped upon it viciously, looking like it was giving the gun the most god-awful fellatio of all time.

"Son of a bitch!" screamed Cliff as he fought the zombie, trying to get his hand on another gun as he fought for his life.

"Cliff? You okay out there, bud?" Ron hollered.

"He's fucking not," said Brandon as he pulled harder on the table.

"You two just get that goddamn door closed!" barked Cliff as he struggled.

"You heard the man, B. Let's haul this shit," said Ron, pushing even harder than before.

It was then that Ron was startled by a pounding on the glass door behind him. Turning, he saw a mangled zombie leading a group of like-minded brain munchers trying to gain entrance into the mall. Still pushing on the table, Ron extended his legs and pressed them on the door to keep the zombies at bay. As the band of undead started pressing harder for entrance, Ron grunted at the pain being brought about by the exertion.

"Fuck this is a bind, B," said Ron through the extra strain.

Brandon looked under the half-closed barrier, eyes widening at what he saw. "Whoa and fucking shit all!" he exclaimed, knowing his friend was in trouble. "Hang on, Ron!"

Letting go of the table, Brandon rushed under the barrier. Getting between Ron and the glass door, Brandon pressed his legs against the door as he put his back on Ron. The two pushed at the table as they struggled to free it still. The door began to crack and wane under the zombie's assault as the table started to move grudgingly with extreme effort.

"This is not how I want to go out, cheek to cheek with you, brother," grunted Ron as he pressed against the table.

"Never been in my top ways to go either," growled Brandon as he kept his feet on the door. The zombies looked at him with ravenous eyes as they demanded fresh flesh to-go. One of the undead almost had the glass broken enough to get a hand inside.

"Well quit enjoying the sensation of my ass and think of something," shouted Ron through the exertion.

Looking about, Brandon finally got a notion, though he loved and loathed it equally. "Fine," he stammered before reaching back and grabbing one of Ron's shotguns. "I wouldn't do this if I didn't think the fucking world of you," he said before aiming the shotgun and pressing with his legs. "Now push!"

As the two friends pressed for all they were worth, Brandon fired the shotgun just as one of the zombies broke through the door. The shotgun blast took the zombie's head clean off. The recoil of the blast, coupled with the exertion on the table, was enough to finally get it moving. Ron's gasped at the sudden release as he ducked his head to not get clobbered. The custodian passed under the barrier, landing safely on the floor as Brandon hit the barrier and crashed on the ground.

Brandon had little other choice but to fire the shotgun and defend himself as the barrier closed completely with him stuck on the other side with the zombies.

Recovering, Ron turned his head just as the barrier finished closing. "Brandon!" he yelled, clamoring to his feet as he rushed to the barrier, but it was too late. On the other side, he could hear the gun blasts and wails of hungry undead. Ron tried to raise the barrier again to get to Brandon to no avail.

Not far away, Cliff had finally gotten the upper hand with the zombie he was quarreling with. Getting his hands on a fresh clip, he ejected the spent one from the gun in the zombie's mouth. Inserting the new one, he nodded with a grin as he prepped the gun into readiness. The zombie continued to chew and suck away, not realizing that his mock blowjob was about to end with an explosive climax.

Cliff pulled the trigger, and there was a satisfying report. The zombie's head shot back as the contents of its cranium barfed out the back of its head. Convulsing for a moment, the creature then went limp on Cliff as the custodian found himself covered with dead zombie, dark blood, and oozing brain-bits. Grunting at the turn of events, Cliff threw off the dead zombie before standing and rushing back to the barrier.

"What the fuck happened?" demanded Cliff as he looked at Ron.

"Brandon just saved my ass and got this thing closed," said Ron as he pressed against the barrier. "We gotta get this back up and save him. He's stuck out there with a bunch of brain-munchers, man."

"Fuck!" spat Cliff as he ran next to Ron and helped push on the barrier.

Together, the two friends could hear the fight waging on the other side. Their friend was putting up a good fight but his ammo was disappearing fast. The shotgun blasts were replaced by the reports of his handgun, but soon this too disappeared. To their frustration, Ron and Cliff could only get the barrier raised about an inch, which merely made the sounds of battle and Brandon's impending demise more vivid. Brandon cried out then, which only made things worse for the two friends as they lost all hope.

It was then that a strong hand emerged under the barrier, lifting it with the utmost ease. Cliff and Ron backed away from the barrier, drawing their weapons as the barrier protested its raising and lost easily. There standing at the door was a pale-skinned jock of a vampire. Resting on his shoulder was Brandon. Behind them, a female vampire finished toppling the zombies with ease before she entered the mall. With her inside, the jock vampire stepped forward, allowing the barrier to close again.

"Looks like we got here in the nick of fucking time," said the jockish vampire.

"I don't know whether to thank you, open fire, or kiss my own ass goodbye," said Ron.

From atop of the vampire, Brandon held up a hand. "No worries, Ron," he said before pointing dazedly at the vampires. "They are changed, but they are still cool, I promise."

Cliff and Ron lowered their weapons. "Well thank God, cause I could use a break and some good news for a change," said Cliff as he extended a hand to Josh. "It's good to see you again and thanks for the save."

Josh shook Cliff's hand gently. "Hey, I couldn't have those dicks munching on my main man here," he said before pointing around the mall. "When Brandon didn't come back, we figured something went down and came looking for him."

"Glad you did," said Brandon dreamily.

"Is he okay?" Ron asked about Brandon.

"He'll be fine," said Josh as he set Brandon down.

"I assume you know how he is around blood," added Sarah.

"Oh, the revelation's become painfully fucking clear as of late," said Ron.

"Hey," said Brandon as he tried to sit up. "I'm getting better. Sorta."

"Yeah, sure, champ," said Josh chuckling at his best bud. "You didn't pass out this time, so I guess I'll give you that," he said.

"Yay me," breathed Brandon as he slumped back on the ground.

"What's the situation?" asked Joshua.

Cliff balled his fists on his hips as he looked around the mall. "Shit's gone to hell in a handbasket. People started turning into zombies and other things and all hell's officially broken loose. We've got most of the zombies taken care of inside the mall, but we need to clean house in here first before we even consider going outside," he said.

Josh nodded. "Yeah, it ain't much better out there. I'd stay in here too if I were you. It's only gotten more boned out there and you humans are a bit squishy," he said.

"You've been a vampire for what, 12 hours now?" Brandon piped in.

"Which is 12 hours longer than you," said Josh. "You guys stay inside and me and Sarah will see what we can do about cleaning up outside."

Cliff nodded. "Sounds good. You have our thanks," he said, pointing to Brandon. "We'll keep him safe until you get back."

Josh nodded. "Thanks. Best wipe him off a bit so he can go back to normal…or as close to normal as you can get him," he said.

"I love you too, you asshole," mumbled Brandon.

"See you soon, love," said Sarah to Brandon before she lifted the barrier and ventured outside with her boyfriend.

"Aren't they just great?" said Brandon to no one in particular. "This almost makes up for the insanity earlier at home. And the damage to the apartment. The loss of our deposit. And the kidnapping of a dickish neighbor. On second thought this is a down payment to making things right. Yeah, that's it. So, what now, guys? I'm just…yeah," he breathed.

Ron leaned over then, grabbing Brandon by his shirt and hauling him to his feet before slapping him around a bit. "God damnit, son, get back in the saddle," he said.

Brandon threw up his hands, stopping the assault. "Wait, wait, wait," he commanded. As Ron stopped, Brandon looked off in the distance, welled in thought. “Nope, better give me one more,” he added.

“Sure thing, buddy,” said Ron, happily obliging and smacking Brandon once more.

Shaking his head clear, Brandon nodded and smiled. “That did it. Thanks, Ron,” he said.

“You kidding? I’ll gash myself up a bit if it means I can do this again in the future,” said his friend.

“God damnit, Ron,” said Brandon before he handed him back his shotgun.

The three friends then began a search of the mall for their comrades. Their progress this time was smoother, much to their approval. Only one zombie reared its head, and it was a head that Ron was more than happy to blow the fuck clean off a set of shoulders shoulders. With steady progress under their belts, they were back upstairs in no time at all.

“Where do you think David got off too?” Brandon mused.

“You never know with that swingin’ dick,” observed Ron.

“I say we just follow this trail of zombie corpses,” said Cliff.

“Just yell out David wrong. He’ll home in on that shit to correct us faster than a bowling ball down a snot slide,” said Ron.

“Let’s not bring unnecessary attention to our position,” ordered Cliff.

“Fine. Go on and take all my fun,” said Ron.

With a little more pushing, the three of them followed the trail of undead to one of the bathrooms. Entering cautiously, the trio got their answer and then some. The bathroom was an infusion of chaos, corpses, and something they could only characterize as sexual confrontation. But there, laid out upon the floor was their friend David Roma.

"Well gawd damn, you won't see that every day," breathed Ron.

David had obviously gone out in a blaze of glory. A broken sword remained lodged in a felled zombie. In the corner rested his empty firearm. Torn clothes were spilled across the bathroom, much of it his, the rest belonged to the woman underneath David's mostly naked body. David appeared to have perished mid-bone, slipping off to his maker on a wave of coital bliss. His naked ass was lost in one final thrust. A trail of blood etched from the bite wound on his head.

Beneath David, the group recognized Janette, obviously a zombie, who was also dead. She appeared to have put up a hell of a fight to eat David, yet the much lover had fought just as hard to have sex with her. Despite the symphony of lusty carnage, Janette's arms and legs were wrapped around David. Somehow the scene was somehow sweet, horrific, and majorly twisted.

"I don't think I have the words," said Brandon.

"You and me both," said Ron.

Cliff nodded solemnly. "Looks like our friend chose to go in a blaze of his preferred glory," he said.

"I pity and admire the sumbitch equally," offered Ron.

"Well, if you gotta go, may as well go out with a bang," noted Brandon as he looked between Cliff and Ron. "Should we, you know, do something?"

Cliff shook his head. "No. He'd want us to leave him like this, I think, so the world can know he went out with a fuck while giving no fucks, so to speak."

"Fair enough," said Brandon.

"Besides," added Ron. "What the hell are you gonna do other than pass the fuck out anyhow?"

Brandon sighed. “I love you, Ron. But also fuck you,” he said.

“I think this bathroom’s stained with enough of that already,” replied Ron.

“Not a literal fuck, Ron. My love only goes so far and is kept on the heterosexual plane,” said Brandon.

“Hey, these are the end of times brother. In another couple weeks, I just might look as sweet as Skittles to you, son. Then we can sit down and deal with the questions you have toward your own sexuality.”

“God, god, god damnit, Ron,” mumbled Brandon.

The three friends were then distracted by repeated and consistent drumming sounds. Readying their weapons again, the three ventured out of the bathroom. Instantly the three of them focused on the source of the noise as he stamped his foot upon the floor. There in a bloodied and poorly tailored suit was Douglas Whitmore, owner of the mall. He looked like a fat man having a controlled temper tantrum as he waited for them impatiently. Brandon and the custodians exchanged glances as they realized the score. Mr. Whitmore was here for them and he was hungry.

And also, he was a dick.

"You boys have gone to great lengths to wreak havoc in my mall," said Mr. Whitworth as he eyed each of them like a slab of meat on a buffet line. He licked his lips lustily, obviously horny for blood.

"Someone had to clean the foxes out of the hen house, and I think we all can agree your fat ass wasn't going to be on that train," yelled Ron back at him.

"What the hell do you want?" asked Cliff warily.

Mr. Whitworth pointed to their feet. "You know what I want. You've delayed this long enough. On your knees.

Pledge your loyalty to me and two of you live today," he said.

"And the third?" asked Brandon.

Douglas shrugged unapologetically. "I'm hungry. It can't be helped. They will be an example made for the other two," replied Mr. Douglas.

Brandon shook his head. "I am afraid that doesn't work for us, Mr. Whitworth. You see, we are a package deal."

"Who all think you are a shady lump of skunk shit," said Ron.

"I think," started Cliff as he tried to sound reasonable, "my friends here are saying that we will have to decline your offer and be on our way. If you can't accept that, then you can expect a quarrel."

Mr. Whitworth grinned. "You don't quarrel with a god, mongrel. You kneel before them or you get squashed under their heel," he declared.

"Wow. And I thought you were a dick before," said Ron.

"That's good. Keep hacking him off, Ron," said Brandon.

"Well he's a dick," countered Ron.

"And I am not offering any guff to that, man, I'm just saying that until we figure out how to kill him, maybe you should dial it down a notch or six," whispered Brandon.

"Buzzkill," mumbled Ron.

"I'm pretty sure our deaths would be the killer of the buzz in this situation."

"Fucking details," said Ron.

"God damnit, Ron," said Brandon.

"Chill, you two," said Cliff as he motioned for them to pipe the fuck down. He then spoke to Mr. Whitworth again. "You are no god, sir. Sure, you have powers now, but do you know how long they will last? Do you know what limits you have? And are you that quick to tempt the fates? I have never known you to be a brave man, always sending people to do the dirty work for you."

Mr. Whitworth nodded triumphantly. "Funny you should say that," he said as he walked to the corner store, ripping open the door. As he did a slew of the hacked off undead poured from it, apparently having no interest in the vampire. Mr. Whitworth pointed in the direction of Brandon and his friends. "Feed," he commanded.

"Feed," came a resounding affirmation as they clamored to the thrill and promise of fresh meat.

"We called it, you cowardly sumbitch!" challenged Ron.

Shaking his head, Brandon spoke to Ron as he prepared to fight again. "Ron, I'm going to guess when you play RPG's and stuff that you are often the tank, cause, man, you are a fucking boss when it comes to drawing aggro," he said.

"You gotta take what god gave you and work it," said Ron as he pumped his shotgun.

As Brandon and his friends prepared for the wave of zombies, raspy yells came from behind them. Turning, they noticed more zombies drawn to the commotion. Swearing to themselves, they went back to back as they forced themselves to hold their fire until it counted. Each bullet was now more precious than the last and it was clear they likely didn't have enough for this onslaught.

"Any thoughts?" Cliff asked through gritted teeth.

"You mean other than the fact that we be fucked?" observed Ron.

"Yeah, Ron. I think that is what he meant," said Brandon.

"So, you have a thought then?" asked Cliff.

Brandon nodded. "Yeah, I think Ron's right. We are definitely fucked."

"Not the way I wanted to start my going out in a blaze of glory," said Cliff as he began to fire at the nearest zombies.

As corpses began to fall, the three friends did their best to keep the hungry undead at bay. Mr. Whitworth smiled ferally as he watched the undead take care of the heavy work. Soon he would swoop in and finish them off, but first there would be fun. He pondered who he would kill first and how he would kill them, deciding to save Ron for last. Mr. Whitworth would savor every moment of the torturous feast.

But then a chilling howl cut through the fantasy as he was forced to gaze beyond his prey.

At the sound of the howl, Cliff smiled as he looked between the zombies in his view. "Well there's something else you don't see every fucking day," he said.

Ron and Brandon chanced a glance too before Ron offered a genuine shit-eatin' grin. "Well gawd damn," he breathed happily.

The three friends watched as what appeared to be a large, panting werewolf charged toward them. The remnants of its clothes indicated that it was their acquaintance Randal. On his back were their friends Dennis and Michael. Michael pointed forward, urging the wolf onward as he tugged at one of two strings that were clearly tied to the wolf's nether regions. Obviously, Randal's harry unmentionables were being used somehow to keep him in check to great effect.

As the neared, Michael shouted his orders. "Alright, Randal! Time to earn your freedom. Let's clean house!"

"You heard the man," said Dennis as he slapped at Randal's hindquarters. "Get to it!"

The werewolf under them mumbled something angrily before he did as he was instructed. Randal ran through the thick of the zombies, slashing and biting as he did. Dennis happily unloaded with his assault rifle before jumping off and assisting Brandon and the others. Joining his friends, Dennis took the bag off his back and placed it between the others.

"Thought you all might be low, so I brought you treats," he said as he unzipped the bag and revealed fresh ammo.

"Oh, you are gonna get a big kiss later, big boy," said Ron merrily.

"There better be tongue and ass-grabbing," replied Dennis as he covered his friends.

As Dennis helped their friends, Michael pushed Randal to tear through the undead like Taco Bell through an unsuspecting colon. The zombies soon gave notice, no longer chasing for blood and brains as they got the hell out of the way. With the path clear, Michael set his sights on Mr. Whitworth as he pointed to the man. Whitworth urged him forward, angered by the intervention and delay to his tortuous feast.

Leaning forward, Michael spoke to Randal. "Well this is for all the marbles, which right now are yours," he stated.

"Rassrole," huffed Randal.

"That a boy," said Michael as he tugged on the twine again. "Now sic'em."

Howling, Randal raced forward as the vampire before him bared his fangs. Michael remained silent and stoic upon Randal's back as they rushed at tremendous speed. With only feet to spare, Michael leaped from Randal, hitting the ground and slowing himself as he rolled. Randal then snarled viciously as he leaped at his target. But even this vaunted bravado faded as he was reminded of the twine and yipped.

Still, Randal was moving quickly and was mid-air as he crashed into Mr. Whitworth. The werewolf's momentum and strength were enough to drive the vampire back. The two men crashed through the barrier railing before falling two floors down. Upon a painful sounding landing, their scuffle resumed. Yet this fight was brief as a tremendous explosion resonated from below before silence descended on the mall.

Standing, Michael chanced a glance below. "Ouch," he said before he removed the twine from his fingers and joined the others.

As Michael neared, the custodians offered each other handshakes and backslapping hugs as they took turns ruffling Brandon's hair. Cliff finally placed his hands on a shoulder of both Dennis and Michael. "We are sure glad to see you guys," he offered before motioning to where Randal had just taken an involuntary dive. "You mind telling us what that was all about?"

Dennis motioned over his shoulder at the carnage that had been wrought behind them. "Oh that? Well let's just say ol'Randal didn't mesh well with the zombie bite and wolfed-out big time. Then he wanted to unload a bunch of unresolved issues on us before we finally got him under control," he said.

"I see," said Cliff. "And what was that I saw? Some grenades attached to his genitals?"

Michael shrugged easily. "If you want to keep a dog in line, a good way is to threaten to neuter it," he replied. "Besides, he sure came in handy just now."

"You mean before you sent him to his explosive death?" asked Brandon.

"Well he was trying to kill us before," said Dennis.

"And, let's face it, he was an asshole," added Michael.

"Didn't like that salty flop of cow shit from the start," replied Ron.

"In all likelihood it was him or us, Brandon," said Cliff knowingly.

"So, what you are saying is that homicide is okay, so long as it is justified?" asked Brandon.

"Exactly," said his four friends in near unison and without hesitation.

Brandon shook his head. "Cool. Just wanted to make sure we were all on the same page and all," said Brandon.

Ron gave him a hearty slap on his back. "That's the spirit, B. You'll be an honorary Fussduster in no time."

Brandon raised an eyebrow. "A Fussduster, huh?"

Ron nodded. "Well hell yeah. I mean, after a post-apocalyptic event, who the fuck are you gonna call? I'd say we have found our calling in life."

Cliff walked away from the conversation, motioning for the others to follow. "Let's go, fellas. Our work isn't done yet," he said before pointing to Brandon. "And don't encourage him."

"Trust me, I'm always trying not to," said Brandon.

Ron soon caught up with the others. "And don't you fuckers shower me with hate till I tell you my plans for the uniforms," he said.

"God damnit, Ron," said the others in perfect unison.

The five comrades made their way slowly and cautiously down to the ground floor once again. Now clear of zombies at least for the moment, they set their intent upon the fat fuck of a blood sucker that remained. There was no love for Mr. Whitworth before he was a vampire and the transformation had merely roided out the sentiment tenfold. The unspoken consensus amongst the five friends was that the owner of the mall had to go, once and for fucking all.

Dead or deader.

If that's even a thing.

Fucking details.

Reaching the ground floor, the group spread out and surrounded where the mall owner lay. The fall had placed Mr. Whitworth and Randal into the scenic fountain that rested below. The subsequent explosion had blown the shit out of said fountain and sent Randal, well, a bit everywhere. Mr.

Whitworth laid in the broken remnants of the fountain, now covered with burns, shrapnel, and lots of bits that were once Randal. His eyes blazed with fury as if being in such a situation was beneath him and too much for his brain to process.

Training his handguns on Mr. Whitworth, Cliff let his voice boom through the lower level of the mall. “Mr. Whitworth, I think it’s time we had a talk,” he said.

Ron quickly chimed in. “You got two choices here, fucker, the easy way and the hard way. Easy you give up and we put you out of your misery. The hard way we kick your ass and then put out of your misery. What’s it gonna be?”

“Very subtle, Ron,” said Brandon.

“It’s a talent,” said Ron.

Slowly, Mr. Whitworth stood and walked from the shattered fountain. Werewolf blood leaked onto the floor along with fountain water and loose change. The explosion had blown open Mr. Whitworth’s shirt, much to the dismay of Brandon and the others. Excess flab was now free for the world to see, looking still like it too was chiseled out of marble. The sight sickened his enemies more than the werewolf bits.

“Cliff,” said Brandon absently, still looking at the train wreck of an image before him. “While I have no desire to die, I still may need you to gouge out my eyes when this is over.”

“Only if you return the favor,” said Cliff.

Mr. Whitworth rubbed at his belly, somehow relishing the sensation. The action nauseated the others, who did their best to hold their resolve. “It is settled then. There are no followers here, only fodder for the feast,” he proclaimed.

“Hard pass, fucknuts,” said Ron.

Michael drew an arrow and trained it on Mr. Whitworth with his bow. “You don’t need followers where you are heading. There's a special place in hell for shit bags like you."

"It shall be fun watching you all die, slowly," said Mr. Whitworth.

"Only way you are getting fangs in me is if it is in my sweet, sweet, ass," said Ron easily. "Cause you can kiss it in its entirety."

"He does have a sweet ass," said Dennis.

"You two have an interesting relationship," said Brandon.

"We just crush a lot," said Ron.

Mr. Whitworth bared his fangs then. "Who's first?"

"Let him have it!" commanded Cliff as the group opened fire.

The group of friends unloaded with everything they had. A steady hail of bullets flooded Mr. Whitworth, causing him to stagger through the sheer intensity. Mr. Whitworth held up his hands, shielding his face as he stumbled back from the assault. Brandon and the custodians continued to fire, not easing until their ammo was all but spent. Lowering their weapons, they paused to see the results of their work.

Ron was able to sum the results with two words. "Well shit," he said.

As the smoke cleared, it was clear that Mr. Whitworth was still standing. To make matters worse, he was even closer to naked than before as he marveled at his own body. The sight sent a shiver through the group as they tried to keep down the contents of their stomachs. Finally, Mr. Whitworth smiled as he realized just how powerful he had become.

Cliff dropped his spent guns as he procured two more. "Hit him with whatever you got and make'em count," he ordered before firing again.

To their surprise, Mr. Whitworth then moved like a lightning bolt, passing by Brandon and the custodians one at a time. They could not see it fast enough to register, but Whitworth struck them all once, sending them flying or falling like sacks of bricks. Before the last one hit the ground, Mr. Whitworth had returned to his starting point, marveling again at his growing powers. This, coupled with his exposed flesh, was enough to give him a serious chubby.

Shaking his head clear and rubbing at his chin, Brandon tried to find his feet again. “Any thoughts, guys?” he asked.

“Don’t look at the fucker’s crotch,” said Ron, wiping blood from his nose.

“I looked at his crotch, Ron,” said Dennis in a haze. “Death can take me in its sweet embrace now.”

“Someone, quick! Make fun of the size of his genitals,” said Michael.

“Not even gonna look at those saggy toilet dippers,” said Ron with a shiver.

“Focus, guys!” said Cliff.

Mr. Whitworth walked over to Cliff and grabbed him by the throat before lifting the man into the air. “I think I will start with you,” he said.

“Oh, hells no,” said Ron as he tried to find his feet.

Seeing Cliff in trouble, Brandon found a surge of energy. It was then in a moment of clarity he realized how to help his friend, though also he realized it was going to suck. Like a lot. Ripping at the bandage on his hand, Brandon struck it with his other hand, letting the blood run again as he did his best to swallow down his disgust. Wiping the blood on both hands, he focused solely on Mr. Whitworth and charged.

As Mr. Whitworth began to squeeze upon Cliff’s neck, Brandon leaped upon his back. Brandon grunted at the impact for it was like straddling a rock. Focusing on the pain and Mr. Whitworth, Brandon ran his bloody fingers into Whitworth’s eyes. Smearing the blood and pressing for all he was worth,

Brandon continued as Whitworth howled, releasing Cliff. As Cliff escaped, Mr. Whitworth spun his body, sending Brandon crashing into a nearby wall.

"You little bastard," spat Mr. Whitworth as he wiped at his eyes. "Don't any of you fools see? You can't stop me! All you can do is piss me off!" he claimed as he walked toward Brandon. "I've changed my mind. You die first." He then took a moment to loom over Brandon as he slowly reached down to claim him.

"I fucking think not," said an angered voice.

Turning toward that familiar voice, Mr. Whitworth saw Brandon's brother Aaron standing with Shawna. Immediately he was torn, for he wanted to kill them too. The look on Aaron's face and the fact that both he and Shawna reeked of sex infuriated him to no end. Screaming his madness, Mr. Whitworth charged, wanting nothing more than to kill Aaron and bang Shawna.

And then probably kill her too.

He tended to handle rejection poorly.

Aaron held out his hands as he focused on Mr. Whitworth. "I may be a piece of shit most of the time but no one, and I fucking mean no one, messes with my brother," he claimed before channeling his will on Whitworth.

Aaron pushed with everything he had, pressing his new powers to the limit. Mr. Whitworth suddenly felt as if he had slammed into a wall, now forced to fight for every inch forward. The vampire growled as he struggled, holding his hands out and fixating on Aaron's neck. This time Aaron held nothing back and slowed Whitworth down to a snail's pace.

As he continued to press, Shawna ran forward, aiming her own hands at the fat fuck before her. Soon a fiery wave of vengeful flame shot from her fingers and enveloped Mr. Whitworth. Mr. Whitworth wailed as the last remnants of his clothing burned off. He shielded his eyes as the flame intensified. Shawna appeared to have no trouble channeling her full anger upon the mall owner.

Lowering her hands, Shawna's eyes gawked at the naked and grotesquely large man in her way. Mr. Whitworth's eyes were shrouded with ferocity and madness as he pushed toward her with slow madness. Behind her, Aaron strained to keep him in place as Brandon and the custodians recovered. From the look etched upon his face, it was clear Whitworth was not stopping until everything in his vicinity was eaten, fucked, or both.

"One way or the other, I'll have you, bitch," growled Mr. Whitworth as he aimed his hands and budding erection fully toward Shawna.

Shawna's eyes set ablaze moments before her hair followed suit. "Well come and get it, baby," she said as a torrent of flame rushed to her hand.

Tired of his shit, Shawna ran at Mr. Whitworth, hand cocked and full of flame. As she got within Whitworth's grabbing distance, Shawna launched her fiery hand between his legs, grabbing fearlessly at his saggy testicles. As she made contact, the flames surged, burning what was in her hand. Mr. Whitworth bellowed a symphony of displeasure as the mall was filled with the unpleasant aroma of roasted nuts.

The pain wrought by toasted testicles allowed Mr. Whitworth to fight through Aaron's strength. Getting one hand up, he struck Shawna, sending her backwards where she landed upon the ground unmoving. Whitworth then breathed a sigh of relief, relishing cool air returning to his nether regions. He took a moment to savor this, uncaring of the telekinetic strength pressing upon him.

Of course, now, Aaron Morgan was beyond pissed.

"YOU DONE FUCKED UP NOW, YOU FUCKING FUCK OF A FUCK!" yelled Aaron as he really set himself to whooping that ass.

Giving it everything he had and then some, Aaron lifted Mr. Whitworth with his mind, flinging and slamming him against several walls, strong enough to shake the mall with the assaults. He then smacked Whitworth upon the ground again, using his strength to hold him in place once more. The exertion was starting to wear on him, and he could feel his powers waning. Sensing this, Mr. Whitworth tried to rush him again.

Finding his feet again, Brandon saw his brother weakening. He pointed to Mr. Whitworth as he roused the custodians. "It's now or never, guys. Let's finish this!"

At his words, the four custodians rushed Mr. Whitworth. Cliff wrapped his arms around the vampire's neck and Ron and Michael grabbed one of his legs a piece as Dennis latched on to an arm. Coupled with Aaron's superpowers, the group was able to halt Whitworth's advance completely. Mr. Whitworth snarled as he tried to move his limbs and bite at the custodians.

"If you got a plan, do it now, B," yelled Ron as he held on for dear life. "I can't be this close to charred, saggy man balls for long!"

Brandon looked around, desperately needing a good idea. Frantic, he at last set his gaze on Cliff's back and decided he had nothing to lose. Running behind Mr. Whitworth and Cliff, Brandon grabbed and unsheathed the sword Cliff had resting there. Taking it in both hands, Brandon geared himself for the task before running past Mr. Whitworth and the custodians.

Stopping, Brandon turned on his heel and clenched to the sword that Warcraft nerds knew as Frostmourne. With Mr.

Whitworth distracted by the others, Brandon ran toward him and leaped. Upon seeing his intentions, Cliff released the vampire's neck and lowered himself. As he flew by the vampire, Brandon slashed once before landing and slowing himself. Behind him, Mr. Whitworth paused, looking forward with eyes horrified with revelation. Utter disbelief took hold of him as his struggle with the custodians ended.

His head then fell clean off and on to Ron's lap.

The custodians released Mr. Whitworth as Ron fumbled with the severed head. Flinging it into the fountain, Mr. Whitworth's head looked at his body as it lumbered a few steps and collapsed. Twitching a few more times, the body went limp as the head tried to utter its protest at the death that had just claimed it.

And then Mr. Whitworth was dead.

Lowering the sword, Brandon breathed a pure and joyous sigh of relief. "Thank the fucking merry maker, it's over," he said.

Standing, Ron gave him a thumbs up. "Nice slicing and dicing, B," he said.

"Yeah, nice work," said Cliff.

Brandon then turned to face his brother. Lowering his hands, Aaron looked beyond exhausted, yet relieved that Brandon was alright. The two brothers exchanged a warm smile and nod. No words were needed between them.

"Ooooooh shit," said Ron then, destroying the victorious calm they had earned with Mr. Whitworth's death.

The others turned to look at what Ron was witnessing. There on her knees was Shawna, shaking violently as she looked at the corpse of Mr. Whitworth. Her fists were clenched now as smoke began to rise from her hands. Her fury was soon matched by the fires wrought from her powers. The temperature around her slowly rose like a fever.

"He was mine. I was supposed to kill him," uttered Shawna as her shaking increased. "I owed that fat fuck."

Aaron slowly approached her. "It's over, baby. We got him together," he offered.

Shawna looked at him with fear and fury in her eyes. "You don't understand. I don't know how much longer I can control these powers. I wanted a win. I wanted to end him, needed to end him. And now that chance is gone," she said.

"Well if you wanna haul off and flambé his fat ass, go right ahead. We'll get the marshmallows," offered Ron.

"He's dead!" Shawna shrieked as she slammed her fist to the ground. As she did, both fists burst into flames. Soon Shawna was covered completely in flame, unable to control or hold back any longer.

As Brandon backed away with the custodians, he spoke to his brother. "I think this is your show, Aaron," he said.

"What the fuck am I supposed to do about this?" pleaded Aaron.

Brandon nodded to his brother. "What you have always wanted to do with Shawna. Love her, man. She needs you now more than ever."

Reluctantly, Aaron nodded. "Alright, man. I'll do what I can. You better steer clear," he said.

Brandon squeezed his brother's shoulder. "I'll be close by," he said before he rushed off to find cover.

Aaron took cautious steps toward Shawna, who was quickly spiraling out of control with her powers. "Baby, listen to me. It's over. We did it. Let's move on past this now," he said.

Shawna shook her head adamantly. "You don't understand. You can't understand. My emotions are linked to my powers. I can't hold it in anymore. All I feel is anger now," she uttered as her body shook more fiercely.

"I don't fucking believe that. Not for one second," countered Aaron as he inched closer. That wasn't anger we shared in that office. That was love. And if you loved me then I know you love me now. Come back to me, baby."

"I can't!" screamed Shawna as she burst completely into flames.

Aaron willed his powers before him, shielding himself from Shawna's unrelenting fury. Still the fires bled warmth through his defense and he immediately broke into sweat. Soon the fires that consumed Shawna rose in a powerful wave around her as she lowered her head and trembled. It was hard to see her now through the flame.

Aaron walked slowly forward, refusing to give up. "I'm not giving up on you. I made that mistake once. You can bet your beautiful ass I won't be doing that ever again!"

Through the flame he heard her. "Run, Aaron. Get away from me. All I have left is this anger. And the flames."

"Like fucking hell that's all you have!" Aaron yelled back in his defense. "You got me! You are stuck with me and that is final."

"It's over," said Shawna bitterly. "This is it. Walk away."

Aaron pressed harder, getting even closer. He could see her shapely silhouette through the flames. "This is not it. I won't give up or quit on you. Not now or ever again," he said.

"Why?!" she demanded.

Aaron enveloped himself in his mental shield, reaching out his hands to cup her cheeks. "Cause I fucking love you, woman!" he declared before kissing her deeply.

The flames singed him, but Aaron did not stop. His lips, pressing to Shawna's, refused to be denied. Slowly the flames subsided as her lips meshed with his. The kiss extinguished all doubt in that moment as the fires that consumed Shawna all but fell away. The kiss lasted long moments after the fires were gone, igniting deeper fires within them both.

At last, Aaron relinquished the kiss to look at her. "Did you hear me? I love you. And that is just how it's going to be no matter what," he said.

Shawna touched his face, looking at him with piercing eyes full of longing and love. "Baby, I love you too," she whispered.

"Then let's make a future together…finally," he replied.

It was then, as she smiled at him that the flames slowly started to return to her eyes and hair. Aaron sucked in a nervous breath as he instinctively protected himself. A burst of flame knocked him back as Shawna fought the emotions swelling within her. She was tired of fighting, tired of the flame that would not be denied.

"NO!" she screamed.

"Shawna!" called out Aaron.

It was then that Shawna looked up to the ceiling. Raising her hands, she allowed her powers to take her. Still soaked in flame, she rose into the air. Fire shot forth, melting a portion of the ceiling as she burst through it. Aaron called out for her again, wanting nothing more than to follow the woman that had a vice grip on his heart.

But soon she was gone, leaving Aaron alone in a beat-up mall with his brother and a handful of custodian friends.

14

THE TIMES, THEY IS A'CHANGING

Brandon and his friends relished the relative safety now offered to them. With the help of Joshua and Sarah, the mall was cleaned of anything that wished to eat, maul, and/or hump them. Days passed stubbornly, and the world that Brandon and his friends knew changed completely. And without venturing outside the mall, the group knew the change was much like the majority of movie reboots in Hollywood. Shitty.

Some of the news of the outside world was acquired through failing media outlets, but it was apparent that no one was untouched by the unfolding insanity. Within days, most television and radio stations went dark. Not long after that, the electricity followed. What started out as a world-spanning party and fuck you to the end was now chock full of the regrets that came in the morning after.

Mankind had fucked itself. And not in the good way. And there was no unfucking it now.

Now, standing outside of the mall on a somberly quiet and sunny Tuesday, Brandon and his friends paid their respects to their fallen friends as they all prepared for the next chapters in their lives. They had procured the last of the alcohol and supplies they could muster and had one final drink together. There had been musings and talks over the last few days about everyone's direction, and unfortunately the decision put the group on different paths.

Holding up his shot of whiskey, Brandon nodded to the grave of David Roma before he knocked it back. Grimacing, he tossed the empty glass before turning to his custodian friends. Each of them was geared for travel, proudly wearing their uniforms. Brandon smiled at them warmly, musing that if the Ghostbusters and Mad Max movies had fucked, their get-up would have been their bastard child.

Brandon extended his hand to Cliff and the two exchanged a deep shake. "You guys sure about this?" he asked.

Cliff nodded, offering a sage-like grin. "We're sure. I feel like we can do some good out here. There are going to be good people in need of help, and we're good at being custodians," he said.

"Fussdusters now, ya'll. Squad for life," offered Ron.

"God damnit, Ron," said Cliff.

"And what about you, boss?" asked Brandon to Jim.

Jim, while not in the uniform of a Fussduster, looked equally ready for travel as he rubbed some sunscreen on his face. "Well I don't know about you, my friend, but I think it's time I retire and see the world. I will stay with these guys until I find the spot I want to call home," he said before chuckling. "I suppose that means you're fired, Brandon," he added.

"Fair enough on all accounts," replied Brandon before he looked past Cliff to his brother Aaron. "Well I still can't believe you're going with them," he said.

Aaron, looking uncomfortable in his borrowed custodian uniform, shrugged as he adjusted his loaded backpack. "Yeah. I got to, man. Shawna's still out there somewhere. I wager if I hang around with these guys, I'll find her again," he said.

Brandon patted his chest. "I can dig it, bro," he said before he walked to Aaron and hugged him. "You be safe out there. And you look after these guys," he said before beholding the others. "And you all look after him."

"Are you going to be okay?" Aaron asked his brother.

Releasing Aaron, Brandon nodded as he motioned behind him. "Yeah. I'll be fine. Besides, someone must look after those two," he said, smiling at Joshua and Sarah.

"Like we can't fucking take care of ourselves now that we're vampires," said Josh.

The quick laughter that escaped Brandon was unrestrained in its judgment. "I would like to point out the present state of our apartment and our current need to acquire new accommodations," countered Brandon.

"That was an adjustment period," replied Josh.

"Which means you could end up even worse before it is over," stated Brandon.

Joshua shook his head, looking to his girlfriend. "Why does he gotta try to ruin this for us, babe?" he asked.

Sarah smiled as she put her arms around him. "Cause he loves us, you big dummy," he said.

"So, where do you think you will head?" asked Brandon to the custodians.

Cliff shrugged. "Wherever we go, that's where we will be. Especially if we are needed," he replied.

"Cryptic and wise," said Brandon as he gave Cliff a hug. "I've always respected that about you."

"Hey, save some of that love for me," said Ron as the other custodians joined in on a manly, backslapping group hug.

"I sure am going to miss you guys," said Brandon mid-hug. The polite squeeze to his left butt cheek grounded him a bit and reminded him who all he was hugging. "Yeah, I am gonna miss you too, Dennis," he added.

"Just making sure," said Dennis.

"Well I need to do the same," said Cliff. "You sure you don't want to come with us?"

Brandon shook his head. "I'm good. I know it would be an adventure, but I need to find some stability. Besides, a blood phobia on the open road? I don't see that ending well for me."

"We sure are gonna miss ya," offered Ron.

"Thanks, man. It's mutual," said Brandon.

"And the fun this phobia let us get away with."

"And fuck you and the horse you road in on, Ron," said Brandon grinning.

"If you will miss Ron that much, we can leave him here with you," said Michael.

"No," came the collective response from Brandon, Josh, Sarah, and Dennis.

"Well, I guess it's time then," said Cliff as he looked at his traveling companions. "Are we ready to do some distance?" he asked.

"I suppose, but I still haven't gotten our theme song fully hashed out yet," said Ron.

"God help us when you do," said Cliff as he motioned ahead. "Let's move, people."

As the custodians set forward, the group exchanged hugs and handshakes one last time. Brandon found it hard to let go of his brother. "You finally went and grew up on me," he said.

Aaron shook his head, offering a wry grin. "I suppose it was time. I'll see you around, B," he said before joining the others.

Brandon, Josh, and Sarah watched the walk a bit before Brandon called out again. "Hey, Cliff. Do you think our paths will cross again?" he asked.

Cliff turned and thought about it for a moment. Looking up at the shining sun, he finally smiled and nodded to his friend. "I think the world owes us that much. I'll see you when we do," he said before turning again.

Brandon waved as his friends and brother made their way toward an unknown future on a highly uncertain road. He tried to make peace with that, hoping beyond all hope that their paths would cross again. Brandon was feeling all the feels right now as the goodbye finally hit him fully. This wasn't a normal farewell. Normal had fucked the chickens and flown the coup a few weeks ago. This was all new territory chock full of extreme uncertainty.

Sensing his friend's sadness, Josh put an arm around Brandon. "You'll see them again, bro. I can feel it, man," he said.

Brandon sighed. "If I live that long," he replied.

"That's kind of defeatist don't you think?" Sarah asked.

"Not if I am living with you two," said Brandon.

"What's that supposed to fucking mean?" growled Joshua.

"Let's just say I know what you both are like," said Brandon as he looked between his two friends. "You are freaks in the sack. Your sexual escapades were almost enough to make us lose our deposit before you were endowed with supernatural strength. God knows what will happen now."

"Maybe the experience has mellowed us out," mused Sarah.

Brandon laughed heartily at this. "That is definitely not a smoke I am going to let you blow up my ass," he said.

Joshua rubbed at his chin. "Course, we could always see if we could get you to join the club," he said.

Brandon held up his hands as he walked away from his friends. "Nope! Not going to happen. Not now. Not ever. And not even thought about in passing, so shut it down and lock it the fuck up here and now," said Brandon, shivering at the prospect.

Joshua threw up his hands. "Well how would you know unless you try it?"

Brandon didn't even look back. "Someone has to be the voice of reason in this group," he stated.

"Well if you are a vampire with us, then that will be the new norm and voice," challenged Joshua.

"Just cause you are going to the Darkside doesn't mean I am going to let you take me with you," countered Brandon.

"Is it the blood? It's the blood isn't it? We can blindfold you or something, maybe get you piss drunk. Wonder what booze would do to your blood anyway," said Josh.

"Oh, go fucking suck yourself already," said Brandon as he kept walking.

Josh and Sarah watched their friend go for a moment before Sarah spoke. "Just give him time," she said.

"Yeah, I guess," said Josh.

"He'll come around," she added.

"I suppose you're right," said Josh with a nod.

Silence passed between them as the two lovers contemplated the future. "So, do you think alcohol changes the flavor of blood?" asked Sarah.

"I suppose there is only one way to find out," offered Joshua.

"And I bet he would taste good regardless, being all good-natured and our friend and all," said Sarah.

"Maybe we can trouble him for a pint or something, work our way into it," said Joshua musingly.

Sarah nodded as her perfect, fang-laced smile lit up her face. "Yes. That's it. All we need is time and alcohol. It's all we ever needed for anything in the past."

Suddenly, Brandon's voice filled the air. "I don't know what the fuck you are talking about, but I bet I won't like it!"

"For fuck's sake, man. We're just talking about your future like concerned fucking friends. You don't gotta be a dick about it," said Josh.

"I heavily doubt that!" yelled Brandon still walking away from them.

"Does he know us or what?" asked Sarah proudly.

"One in a million," beamed Josh before he hollered again. "What do you think about some lunch, B? We could go for a bite or a pint if you are feeling generous."

"Why don't you just break off that supernatural cock of yours and go fuck yourself!" replied Brandon.

Josh exchanged a playful glance with his girlfriend. "Yeah, he'll come around," he said before he and Sarah went to catch up with their friend.

THE END.

SORTA.

IT'S ALSO KIND OF THE BEGINNING.

YOU'LL SEE.

THE MISADVENTURES OF BRANDON
AND HIS FRIENDS CONTINUE

IN BOOK TWO,

SO, NOW WHAT?

ABOUT THE AUTHOR

David Partelow was born and raised in Kansas City, Missouri. He is an avid poet, novelist, father, lover of life, sarcasm advocate, connoisseur of all things nerdy, and all around pain in the hind end. And a Scorpio too if you must know. He specializes in science fiction, fantasy and sometimes dabbles in works of comedy. When not writing, he does other stuff and runs on caffeine and denial. Included in this is practicing a Russian Martial Art known as Systema, crafting nerd things, cosplaying, and getting in and out of trouble. For more information you can find him on the below media outlets:

Facebook page: Dabbles and Dorkery
Twitter @thedorkery

If that is still not enough information, let's talk restraining order…

Other Works by David Partelow

LORE: Legacy of Revelation, Earth
The Vallance War Series
Ashener's Calling
Echoes of Ashener
Vallance Rising
Shadow Falls

Crescent Moon
Crescent Moon
Theophilus Thistle Trilogy
The Adventures of Theophilus Thistle
Shaman's Fury
Vow of the Valorous

CPSIA information can be obtained
at www.ICGtesting.com
Printed in the USA
LVHW021222071019
633402LV00002B/445/P

9 781694 845429